William Falconer, Robert Carruthers, Myles Birket Foster

The Shipwreck

A Poem

William Falconer, Robert Carruthers, Myles Birket Foster

The Shipwreck
A Poem

ISBN/EAN: 9783744765435

Printed in Europe, USA, Canada, Australia, Japan

Cover: Foto ©Andreas Hilbeck / pixelio.de

More available books at **www.hansebooks.com**

THE

SHIPWRECK:

A POEM.

BY WILLIAM FALCONER.

WITH LIFE BY ROBERT CARRUTHERS.

Illustrated by Birket Foster.

LONDON:

T. NELSON AND SONS, PATERNOSTER ROW;

EDINBURGH; AND NEW YORK.

1868.

Contents.

List of Illustrations

DESIGNED BY BIRKET FOSTER.

ENGRAVED BY EDMUND EVANS, DALZIEL BROTHERS, AND W. T. GREEN.

CANTO SECOND.

CANTO THIRD.

The Vignettes and Initial Letters designed by NOEL HUMPHREYS,
and engraved by H. N. WOODS.

MEMOIR OF FALCONER.

HAT genius will vindicate its celestial origin, and burst through all obstructions, is an axiom illustrated by many splendid and interesting examples. The energies of an original creative mind and bold imagination can never be wholly repressed or obscured by circumstances: the cloud that carries the electric fire conceals it but for a time, and its manifestations appear all the brighter from the previous gloom. In the list of eminent self-taught men who have shed lustre on our imaginative literature, a high rank must be assigned to the poet of the Shipwreck. No distinguished author ever rose from a lower level, or had to contend with more depressing difficulties. His early years were doomed to hardship, disappointment, and misery; and his situation as a common seaman—"a ship-boy on the high and giddy mast"—precluded nearly all opportunities of literary study or advancement, until after long years of severe and irksome toil. In this respect he stands alone in our annals. Burns, Gifford, Bloomfield, or Hogg, had no such hard ascent to climb. The shepherd on his hill and the rustic at his plough have each a certain range of natural freedom, and chances of intellectual companionship and enjoyment. The mechanic also has his hours of leisure and access to books. None of them are debarred the supreme luxury and elevating influences of Sabbath rest, summer walks, and female society. But the young apprenticed seaman is restricted to one set of associates, often men coarse, ignorant, and boisterous, and is chained to a round of duties and dangers—too frequently enforced with all the tyranny or caprice of arbitrary power—from which there is little intermission and no escape. A love of adventure or a passionate desire to visit foreign countries may sometimes soften the picture and veil its harsher features; but in the case of Falconer there appears to have been no such alluring medium. He entered with strong reluctance on his profession of a sailor, and was only forced into it by utter helplessness and destitution. No other outlet seemed attainable; every gate of hope was shut against him. He therefore submitted, "forlorn of heart," as he tells us, to the "severe decree," and embarked on that faithless and stormy element, from which he was destined ultimately to reap his poetical fame, and in which he found a sad and premature grave.

WILLIAM FALCONER was born in Edinburgh, on the 11th of February 1732. In the parish register his father (who was also named William) is designated a wigmaker; in other accounts he is termed a "poor barber." He was probably both at different periods of his life; but at this time the wigmakers formed a class of respectable burgesses in the Scottish capital. The maiden name of the poet's mother was Agnes Shand, and she was remembered as a careful and exemplary matron, intelligent, industrious, and affectionate. The elder Falconer carried on business in that ancient quarter of the town known as the Netherbow, where stood the once famous "Port" or gate condemned to destruction by the government of George II., in petty and ludicrous resentment of the Porteous Mob of 1736, but which flourished long afterwards with its towers, battlements, and spire. This antique structure extended right across High Street, dividing that most picturesque of city thoroughfares from the privileged and historical district of the Canongate. Shops and houses with wooden fronts and "fore-stairs" were clustered round the Port, and in one of these dwelt William Falconer, a citizen remarkable for his humour and eccentricity, who has been compared to Partridge in "Tom Jones," and who, like that learned and witty tonsor, was somewhat unthrifty and unfortunate. Pity it is that the jest and tale which gladden these little coteries do not always carry prosperity with their sunshine! The merriest man in the Netherbow was one of the most unlucky of its tradesmen. William Falconer became insolvent, and the wig-making establishment was given up. His friends then came to his assistance, and he was enabled to begin business as a grocer. The shop was chiefly superintended by his wife; and on the death of this prudent and excellent partner, the affairs of the old man again became deranged. Recovery was hopeless, and the latter days of William Falconer were passed in extreme indigence. The family of this unfortunate couple consisted of three children: the poet, and a brother and sister, both born deaf and dumb, whose pitiable condition added to the other calamities of the poor household.

The helpless brother and sister found an asylum as pauper-patients in the Edinburgh Infirmary : William, after a little schooling with one Webster, was put to sea. He was then probably not more than twelve or thirteen years of age, but active and eager for the acquisition of knowledge. A love of nature also—the poet's inheritance—came upon him. As a stripling, he said, his bosom "danced to nature's charms." In the course of his foreign wanderings and night-watches he must occasionally have recalled the unique and magnificent features of his native city and its surrounding scenery; but the distressing circumstances of his boyhood could not be recollected without painful emotion, and in his poetry he is silent as to the scene of his birth and childhood.

It is possible that the humble fortunes of the family had not reached their lowest ebb till some years after the birth of the poet. In describing, under the name of Arion, his early attainments and misfortunes, Falconer conveys the impression that he had at least entered upon a liberal course of education :—

> " On him fair science dawned in happier hour,
> Awakening into bloom young fancy's flower ;
> But soon adversity, with freezing blast,
> The blossom withered, and the dawn o'ercast.
> Forlorn of heart, and by severe decree,
> Condemned reluctant to the faithless sea,
> With long farewell he left the laurel grove
> Where science and the tuneful sister's rove."

We have, however, the poet's own statement, made repeatedly to his friend, Governor Hunter, that his education was confined to reading, writing, and a little arithmetic ; and the early age at which he must have left home, added to the straitened circumstances of his parents, may be held as confirmatory of the fact. The farewell to science and the laurel grove was probably, in those days of artificial poetry, deemed necessary and indispensable as an embellishment of the narrative. Falconer was entered apprentice on board a merchant vessel belonging to Leith. The usual period of apprenticeship for a sailor was then four years, but it is doubtful whether Falconer served the whole of this period. Before he had completed his eighteenth year we read of his having exchanged the merchant service for the Royal Navy ; of his wandering, apparently without any fixed employment, through various scenes in the East, and of his engaging himself at the port of Alexandria as a mate on board the *Britannia*, a merchantman engaged in the Levant trade. In the Royal Navy the purser of his ship was

Archibald Campbell, son of Professor Campbell of St. Andrews, and who is known as author of a parody on the style of Dr. Johnson, entitled "Lexiphanes." To this literary purser Falconer acted as servant, and, according to Dr. Currie (the biographer of Burns), Campbell delighted in improving the mind of the young seaman, and afterwards, when the latter had attained celebrity, felt a pride in boasting of his scholar. The period of tuition, however, must have been a brief one; for, in the autumn of 1750, Falconer, then only eighteen, as we have stated, sailed from Alexandria for Venice as second mate of the *Britannia*. Such an appointment for one so young speaks well for his proficiency as a sailor. The British merchantmen at this time, as we learn from Mr. Stanier Clarke, remained trading from port to port in the Levant and Mediterranean, until ordered for England, when they generally loaded with silks at Leghorn. The *Britannia* had "wafted her commercial store" along the shores of Africa and Italy, and, having touched at Alexandria and Crete, sailed for Venice, whence she was to steer for England. The vessel, however, was overtaken by a dreadful storm off Cape Colonna, on the coast of Greece, and suffered shipwreck. The whole of the crew, consisting of about fifty men, perished, with the exception of three of the number, of whom Falconer happily was one. The incidents of the voyage, and its disastrous termination, left an indelible impression on the young sailor's memory; and years afterwards he selected them as the subject of that poem which has rendered his name and misfortunes immortal.

After the wreck of the *Britannia*, and his return to England, Falconer revisited his native city, and there made his first appearance as an author. The death of Frederick, Prince of Wales, in March 1751, called forth numerous elegies and lamentations, and among the public mourners was our young poetical mariner. His effusion, printed at Edinburgh, is entitled "A Poem Sacred to the Memory of his Royal Highness Frederick, Prince of Wales." The poem, it must be admitted, was one of the most unpromising of youthful productions. Melpomene has rarely been invoked with less success; for conventional as the poetical style and diction of that period were, such puerile and inflated lines as the following—the best in the piece —are below even the ordinary standard :—

" Oh, bear me to some awful silent glade,
 Where cedars form an unremitting shade ;
 Where never track of human feet was known ;
 Where never cheerful light of Phœbus shone ;

> Where chirping linnets warble tales of love,
> And hoarser winds howl murmuring through the grove ;
> Where some unhappy wretch aye·mourns his doom,
> Deep melancholy wandering through the gloom
> Where solitude and meditation roam,
> And where no dawning glimpse of hope can come !
> Place me in such an unfrequented shade,
> To speak to none but with the mighty dead ;
> To assist the pouring rains with brimful eyes,
> And aid hoarse howling Boreas with my sighs."

The youth and circumstances of the writer form an excuse for such imma-
turity of taste and judgment. But it is curious to find Falconer, many years
afterwards, in the second edition of his Shipwreck, allude with some com-
placency to this first production :—

> " Thou who hast taught the tragic harp to mourn,
> In early youth, o'er royal Frederick's urn."

His desire to appear loyal, and steadfast in his loyalty, had overpowered
his critical perceptions. For about ten years subsequent to this period our
author is supposed to have been engaged in the merchant service. He has
enumerated all the shores he traversed—from the Peruvian regions to savage
Labrador, and from Damascus, "pride of Asian plains," to the Isthmus of
Darien. Adversity, he said, still pursued him, but self-improvement was
not neglected. He picked up acquaintance with the French, Spanish, and
Italian languages ; and he occasionally, when in Britain, sent a copy of
verses to that popular repertory of fugitive literature, the "Gentleman's
Magazine." Some of these pieces have been identified and reprinted. The
best of them are nautical, showing that he had at length struck into the
true path of his genius. The following "Description of a Ninety-gun Ship"
is correct and animated :—

> " Amidst a wood of oaks with canvas leaves,
> Which formed a floating forest on the waves,
> There stood a tower, whose vast stupendous size
> Reared its huge mast, and seemed to gore the skies.
> From which a bloody pendant stretched afar
> Its comet-tail, denouncing ample war :
> Two younger giants,* of inferior height,
> Displayed their sporting streamers to the sight :
> The base below, another island rose,
> To pour Britannia's thunder on her foes :·
> With bulk immense, like Ætna, she surveys
> Above the rest, the lesser Cyclades :

---

* "Younger giants :" fore and mizen masts.

Profuse of gold, in lustre like the sun,
Splendid with regal luxury she shone,
Lavish in wealth, luxuriant in her pride,
Behold the gilded mass exulting ride !
Her curious prow divides the silver waves,
In the salt ooze her radiant sides she laves ;
From stem to stern, her wondrous length survey,
Rising a beauteous Venus from the sea :
Her stem, with naval drapery engraved,
Showed mimic warriors, who the tempest braved ;
Whose visage fierce defied the lashing surge,
Of Gallic pride the emblematic scourge.
Tremendous figures, lo ! her stern displays,
And holds a Pharos* of distinguished blaze :
By night it shines a star of brightest form,
To point her way, and light her through the storm :
See dread engagements pictured to the life,
See admirals maintain the glorious strife :
Here breathing images in painted ire,
Seem for their country's freedom to expire :
Victorious fleets the flying fleets pursue—
Here strikes a ship, and there exults a crew :
A frigate here blows up with hideous glare,
And adds fresh terrors to the bleeding war.
But leaving feigned ornaments, behold !
Eight hundred youths, of heart and sinew bold,
Mount up her shrouds, or to her tops ascend,
Some haul her braces, some her foresail bend ;
Full ninety brazen guns her port-holes fill,
Ready with nitrous magazines to kill ;
From dread embrasures formidably peep,
And seem to threaten ruin to the deep :
On pivots fixed, the well-ranged swivels lie,
Or to point downward, or to brave the sky :
While peteraroes swell with infant rage,
Prepared, though small, with fury to engage.
Thus armed, may Britain long her state maintain,
And with triumphant navies rule the main !"

Not less faithful are the satirical sketches entitled "The Chaplain's Peti-
tion" and "The Midshipman," but they have no great poetical merit. The
admirable naval song of "The Storm" ("Cease, rude Boreas, blustering
railer!"), which the singing of Incledon once made so popular, has been
assigned to Falconer, instead of its reputed author, George Alexander
Stevens. There is a mixture of carelessness and jollity, combined with a
flow of lyrical melody, in this song, which appears to us quite foreign to
Falconer's usual manner. It was certainly easier and more natural for
Stevens, a good song writer and man of imitative talent, to play the sailor,

---

* "Pharos ;" her poop lanthorn.

and import some nautical phrases, than for Falconer to write once, and once only, in a strain different from all his other compositions. We believe, also, that if "The Storm" had been written by our author, he would have acknowledged and claimed it, proud as he was of displaying his naval knowledge and enthusiasm.

From the merchant service Falconer is reported to have re-entered the Royal Navy, and to have been on board the *Ramilies* man-of-war when that ship was wrecked in the Channel near Plymouth, in February 1760. The officers and men of the *Ramilies* numbered 734, and of these only one midshipman and twenty-five seamen were saved. The poet is said to have been the midshipman ;* but we can find no authority for the assertion. Had Falconer sailed with the *Ramilies*, or been preserved a second time from shipwreck, under circumstances so tragic and memorable, he would scarcely have refrained from some allusion to the event in his poetry. We have also the distinct statement of Mr. Clarke, that after the wreck of the *Britannia*, in 1750, Falconer continued in the merchant service until he had gained the patronage of his Royal Highness Edward, Duke of York, by dedicating to him his poem of "The Shipwreck."

That great narrative poem, so truly British in subject and feeling, and so original in execution, appeared in May 1762, in the form of a thin quarto volume, price five shillings. It was illustrated with a chart of the ship's course, and an engraving of the elevation of a merchant ship, with all her masts, yards, sails, and rigging. Such a work was a novelty in what was termed ·polite literature. The descriptive Muse never before appeared in such a nautical costume ! The title-page bore that the volume was "printed for the author," an indication, probably, that the poet had not been able to find a purchaser for the copyright of his work; and it was dedicated, by permission, to the Duke of York, " Rear-Admiral of the Blue Squadron of his Majesty's Fleet." To this dedication—a plain unflattering inscription— Falconer affixed his name. The title of the work was simply "The Shipwreck, a Poem in Three Cantos, by a Sailor," with the motto from Virgil (Æneid, bk. ii. v. 5)—

> ...." quæque ipse miserrima vidi,
> Et quorum pars magna fui."

It is gratifying to find that the royal patron acknowledged the honour conferred upon him, and testified his sense of the merits of the poem by a

---

* " Lives of Scottish Poets." London, 1822.

prompt and substantial mark of regard. He advised Falconer to quit the merchant service and enter the Royal Navy; and, in consequence of the Duke's recommendation and influence, the poet was rated as a midshipman on board Sir Edward Hawke's ship, the *Royal George.* At the same time his poem no less rapidly advanced in popularity. Though only an outline or skeleton of what it was afterwards to become under the hands of its author, the Shipwreck was hailed as one of our finest and most original national poems. Its descriptions were pronounced to be not inferior to those in the Æneid; and, in versifying his sea language, Falconer was held to have achieved a greater miracle of success than that accomplished by Homer, in reducing his catalogue of ships into flowing and sonorous verse. Such exaggerated praise was an error, but it was an error on the right side. It is seldom that the world is too generous to those who minister to its instruction or delight.

This was the happiest period of Falconer's life. He could tread the quarter-deck of the *Royal George* with conscious and justifiable pride. He had won poetical fame, unquestionably the dearest wish of his heart; he had, unsolicited, obtained professional advancement; and he enjoyed the patronage of a young and gallant prince, who had the taste to appreciate and the power to reward his genius. Though long buffeted by adverse gales of fortune, he was only yet in his thirtieth year, still eager to run the race for manly honours; and Hope, that had so often allured and deceived him, might now assume her fairest form and brightest colours. His gloomy forebodings and querulous discontent were all hushed in joy and gratulation. Love, also, was joined to Hope. Falconer's temperament seems to have been grave and serious—perhaps austere. His appearance was not prepossessing, bespeaking the rough sailor rather than the poet. But he had all the poet's warmth and depth of feeling; and his solitary and somewhat rugged nature, when kindled up by contact with a congenial mind, found expression in fluent and impressive speech. Those who have most keenly felt adversity and neglect are soonest melted by kindness and sympathy. The worth and talents of Falconer attracted the notice of a young lady, daughter of the surgeon of Sheerness Yard; an intimacy sprung up between them, though discountenanced by Mr. Hicks, the lady's father; and the charms of "Miranda" called forth some pleasing ballad stanzas from the author of the Shipwreck. In political or satirical verse (which he afterwards attempted) Falconer signally failed; in amatory poetry he had better success, for he wrote from genuine passion and true impulses. Stanzas like the following have rarely proceeded from the *orlop*, or midshipman's cabin :—

ADDRESS TO MIRANDA.

The smiling plains, profusely gay,
Are dressed in all the pride of May ;
The birds on every spray above
To rapture wake the vocal grove.

But, ah ! Miranda, without thee,
Nor spring nor summer smiles on me :
"All lonely in the secret shade,
I mourn thy absence, charming maid !

Oh, soft as love ! as honour fair !
Serenely sweet as vernal air !
Come to my arms ; for you alone
Can all my absence past atone.

Oh, come ! and to my bleeding heart
Thy sovereign balm of love impart :
Thy presence lasting.joy shall bring,
And give the year eternal spring !

We also subjoin the second of these pieces, which, in plaintive tenderness and melody, is equal to the ballad strains of the author's countrymen, Mickle or Mallet :—

THE FOND LOVER.

A BALLAD, WRITTEN AT SEA BY THE AUTHOR OF "THE SHIPWRECK."

A nymph of every charm possessed,
That native virtue gives,
Within my bosom all confessed,
In bright idea lives.
For her my trembling numbers play
Along the pathless deep,
While, sadly social with my lay,
The winds in concert weep.

If beauty's sacred influence charms
The rage of adverse fate ;
Say why the pleasing soft alarms
Such cruel pangs create ?
Since all her thoughts by sense refined,
Unartful truth express ;
Say wherefore sense and truth are joined
To give my soul distress ?

If when her blooming lips I press,
Which vernal fragrance fills,
Through all my veins the sweet excess
In trembling motion thrills ;

Say whence this secret anguish grows,
    Congenial with my joy !
And why the touch, where pleasure glows,
    Should vital peace destroy ?

If, when my fair, in melting song,
    Awakes the vocal lay,
Not all your notes, ye Phocian throng,
    Such pleasing sounds convey ;
Thus wrapt all o'er with fondest love,
    Why heaves this broken sigh ?
For then my blood forgets to move,
    I gaze, adore, and die.

Accept, my charming maid, the strain
    Which you alone inspire ;
To thee the dying strings complain
    That quiver on my lyre.
Oh, give this bleeding bosom ease,
    That knows no joy but thee ;
Teach me thy happy art to please,
    Or deign to love like me.

                                            W. F.

ROYAL GEORGE, *August* 2 [1762].

Before the close of the year the Duke of York sailed again in command
of the fleet, and Falconer, thinking probably, with Gray, that it is "better
that gratitude should sing than expectation," wrote an *Ode on the Duke of
York's Second Departure from England as Rear-Admiral.* "He composed
it," says Governor Hunter, who was then a midshipman in the *Royal George,*
"during an occasional absence from his messmates, when he retired into a
small space formed between the cable-tiers and the ship's side." * Governor
Hunter must have been mistaken in his recollection of the piece thus composed. The Ode was not published till some months after the Duke's
departure, and it is an elaborate production of above two hundred and
thirty lines, in all the intricate variety of metre to be found in Dryden's
great Ode on St. Cecilia's Day, of which it is in some respects an imitation,
though in quality more akin to the early Pindaric attempts of Swift. The
gratitude of the poet is warmly expressed, and in the conclusion of the ode

---

* Mr. Stanier Clarke's Life of Falconer prefixed to Shipwreck, London 1804. Mr.
Clarke states that Falconer's Ode was published on occasion of the Duke of York embarking on board the *Centurion* with Commodore Harrison. But the *Centurion* did not sail
on this expedition till September 1763, and Falconer's poem was published some months
earlier. It was written before the conclusion of the war. The second departure of the
Duke was that in November 1762, when his Royal Highness was associated in the command with Sir Charles Hardy, and "moved to war," as the poet says, "through storms
and wintry seas."

he hints that he may yet be called upon to celebrate some great naval
victory :—

> " Perhaps the chief to whom I sing
>   May yet ordain auspicious days,
>   To wake the lyre with nobler lays,
>   And tune to war the nervous string.
>   For who, untaught in Neptune's school,
>   Though all the powers of genius he possess,
>   Though disciplined by classic rule,
>   With daring pencil can display
>   The fight that thunders on the watery way ;
>   And all its horrid incidents express ?
>   To him, my Muse, these warlike strains belong ;
>   Source of thy hope, and patron of thy song !"

This warlike wish was frustrated by the treaty of peace between Great
Britain, France, and Spain, which was signed at Paris on the 10th of February 1763.

As Falconer could not have obtained further promotion in the Royal
Navy without some years of service, he was advised to exchange into the
civil department ; and in the year 1763 he was appointed purser of the
Glory frigate, 32 guns. The purser, as he himself has stated, is "an officer
appointed by the Lords of the Admiralty to take charge of the provisions
of a ship of war, and to see that they are carefully distributed to the officers
and crew, according to the instructions which he has received from the
Commissioners of the Navy for that purpose." Thus settled, the naval poet
completed his happiness by marrying his "Miranda," who appears to have
been every way worthy of his affection. Mr. Clarke says, "Mrs. Falconer
is described to me as displaying keen abilities ; and that it was the lustre of
her mind rather than of her person which attracted and confirmed the
affection of her husband." A contemporary of the lady, who knew her,
and a man of literary tastes, Mr. Joseph Moser, describes the poet's wife
as "a woman of cultivated mind, elegant in her person, and sensible and
agreeable in conversation."

At this time, or shortly before, Falconer is said to have paid a final visit
to Scotland. Dr. Irving, in a sketch of the poet's life, first mentioned the
fact, adding that Falconer "resided for some time at the manse of Gladsmuir, which was then possessed by his illustrious kinsman, Dr. Robertson.
This great historian, whose father was the cousin-german of old Falconer,
seems to have been proud to acknowledge his relationship to the ingenious
self-taught poet." Dr. Irving, however, is wrong either as to the date of

Falconer's visit or the residence of Dr. Robertson. If the former took place, as he states, after the publication of the Shipwreck, the poet must have met his kinsman in Edinburgh, for Robertson left Gladsmuir in 1758. The meeting most probably took place in the Scottish capital, and each had special cause for congratulation. Robertson, by his first work, the "History of Scotland," had reached the highest popularity: Falconer, by his one poem, had earned scarcely less distinction, overcoming by the force of native genius the difficulties incident to his nautical task, and uniting with his technical lore the inspiration and energy of a true poet. We have no record of the feelings of Falconer on revisiting, at this interesting period, the haunts of his boyhood: the old Netherbow Port and High Street, and the shores of Leith, whence, sad at heart, he had first embarked on the sea. There is usually much disappointment at such reunions. Every object appears less than memory, aided by imagination, had represented it; schoolboy friends are gone, or the few that are left, busy with their own pursuits, seem cold and careless; we look for some cherished object—a house or tree—and it is removed. Time has hastened on, and we forget that its flight effaces the old landmarks. But Falconer had not lived in vain; he had struggled through the past up to worldly honour, and he could look forward into the future without dread, solaced and cheered by domestic happiness.

His fortunes, however, were always fluctuating. After the peace, his ship, the *Glory*, was laid up in ordinary at Chatham, and a purser's half-pay was but a slender provision. At this juncture he found a kind and considerate friend in one of the Commissioners of the Navy, Mr. Hanway, brother of Jonas Hanway, whose controversy with Johnson on the qualities and effects of tea has preserved his name better than his published travels, foreign or domestic. Commissioner Hanway admired the genius of the purser of the *Glory*, and he set about preparing for him an appropriate residence. "The captain's cabin," says Mr. Clarke, "was ordered to be fitted up with a stove, and with every addition of comfort that could be procured, in order that Falconer might thus be enabled to enjoy his favourite propensity (literary occupation) without either molestation or expense."

The first emanation from this marine study was a new edition of the Shipwreck, "corrected and enlarged," which appeared in an octavo volume in 1764, printed not for the author (as in the former instance), but for A. Millar in the Strand. This enlarged edition was almost a new work.

Above nine hundred lines were added, and these included all of what may be called the character-painting of the poem, as the delineations of Albert and Rodmond, and the episode of Palemon. In the " Advertisement " Falconer made this statement :—

" Although it is so frequent a practice to take the advantage of public approbation, and raise the price of performances that have been much encouraged, the author chooses to steer in a quite different channel. It being a considerable time since the first edition sold off (notwithstanding the high price and the singularity of the subject), he might very justly continue the price; but as it deterred a number of the inferior officers of the sea from purchasing it, at their repeated requests it has been printed now in a smaller edition. At the same time the author is sorry to observe that the gentlemen of the sea, for whose entertainment it was chiefly calculated, have hardly made one-tenth of the purchasers."

Falconer, like Arbuthnot, "knew his art but not his trade." He was ambitious of his reputation for professional skill—not covetous of money. Had the latter been his object, he would probably, like his countryman Thomson (though Thomson was only driven to such a step by necessity), or like the earlier Georgian poets, have had recourse to a subscription edition, which his naval friends would, no doubt, have rendered profitable. The next production of our author was a rhyming satire on Lord Chatham, Wilkes, and Churchill, entitled *The Demagogue.* It must have been written after the publication of Churchill's " Gotham " in the spring of 1764, and before the death of that unscrupulous but powerful satirist in November of the same year. Nearly all the literary Scotsmen of that period were engaged in defence of the Bute Administration. It had become a point of honour with them, as the contest seemed to be one, as of old, between the thistle and the rose. Wilkes, Churchill, the Whigs and Dissenters, were against Scotland and Scotsmen. Chatham abjured local and national pre-judices, but he fought on the same side. Never was the Crown or Govern-ment more fiercely assailed than at this time ; and besides nationality of feeling—the *perfervidum ingenium Scotorum* roused by repeated attacks— Falconer was bound, both by gratitude and consistency, to the side of the king's friends. His best patron was the brother of his sovereign, and his first poetical effort was devoted to the cause of royalty. His *Demagogue,* however, was a poor fragmentary performance, remarkable for its virulence and not for its poetry. Of the tact, humour, or wit, essential in political satire, he was destitute—his strength was derived from the sea ; and as the sailor fears to whistle in a storm, Falconer would have best consulted his fame by remaining silent during the noise and fury of the political elements.

The remaining five years of Falconer's life are involved in some obscu-rity. In 1767, according to Mr. Clarke, he was appointed from the *Glory* to the *Swiftsure*—still, we presume, a purser; and then we hear of his having left his naval retreat at Chatham, and of his being obliged to take up his abode in a garret in London, deriving a pittance from writing in the "Critical Review." Why he should have resigned his naval appointment does not appear. He was too practical and too sensible a man to have abandoned a secure and respectable position for the precarious gains of authorship, for which he had no peculiar vocation ; and the death of his patron, the Duke of York (September 17, 1767), could not, we presume, have caused his retirement. The story of the garret is, we suspect, fabulous. It is certain that Falconer could not have struggled long, as Mr. Clarke asserts, against the *res angustæ domus*, for we have only a period of two years between 1767 and his death, and during that time one at least of his most intimate friends did not consider him to be in poverty. A bookseller, Mr. John Murray (grandfather of the present eminent publisher of that name), requested the poet to join him as partner. In a letter, dated October 16, 1768, Mr. Murray writes to Falconer, then at Dover, that a certain Mr. Sandby, bookseller, opposite St. Dunstan's Church, was about to retire from his shop in Fleet Street, and that his business could be obtained for a sum not much beyond £400. "I have little reason," says Mr. Murray, "to fear success by myself in this undertaking, yet I think so many additional advantages would accrue to us both, were your forces and mine joined, that I cannot help mentioning it to you, and making you the offer of entering into company." * The poet, he added, would be assumed as partner on equal terms. This offer proves that Falconer could not have been in the very reduced circumstances in which he is represented by his biographers, and it proves also that he must have possessed the correct and steady habits of a man of business. He seems to have declined the offer, probably because his "Marine Dictionary" was then near completion, and he might reasonably anticipate from its publication some favourable naval appointment. His "Dictionary" appeared in August 1769, dedicated to the Lords Commissioners of the Admiralty. It had engaged his utmost

---

* Mr. Stanier Clarke's Life of Falconer, p. 37.

application, he said, for some years. The undertaking was first suggested to him by his "worthy and ingenious friend," George Lewis Scott, Esq., and its utility had been acknowledged by Sir Edward Hawke, and other naval authorities. In a country deriving its principal sources of strength from the superiority of its marine, such a work was evidently wanted, and Falconer had laboured strenuously to render his Dictionary accurate and complete. All that related to the equipment and movements of a ship, or to the practice of naval war, was derived, he said, chiefly from his own observation; in treating of the artillery he had consulted various authors, and in the part connected with ship-building he acknowledged his obligations to M. Du Hamel—a high authority on naval architecture—who had written to him on the subject of his work in complimentary terms. The Dictionary, we may add, was a large quarto volume, and was illustrated with a variety of original designs of shipping in different situations, with separate views of the masts, sails, &c.

Such an important service could not fail to attract the notice of the Admiralty, and remind them of the strong claims of its author. Accordingly, we find that almost immediately after the publication of his Dictionary, Falconer received an appointment which promised to be the most lucrative and considerable he had yet held. The affairs of India were then in a critical position, in consequence of the wars of Hyder Ali, and of disputed territorial revenues, and the Company resolved on sending out three commissioners or supervisors, invested with extraordinary powers for the emergency. These were, Henry Vansittart, Luke Scrofton, and Colonel Francis Forde. The *Aurora* frigate was selected for the voyage, and Falconer was nominated as purser of the vessel, with a promise that he would also receive the appointment of private secretary to the commissioners.

Before embarking on this mission Falconer prepared a third edition of the Shipwreck. He put his name on the title-page, left out the dedication, and prefixed to the volume an advertisement, stating that he had given the poem a strict and thorough revision, from which he flattered himself that it had received very considerable improvements. He was then living in Somerset House, from which this intimation is dated, October 1, 1769— the day preceding his departure from England. About two hundred new lines were added to the poem, and its general arrangement was improved. Favourite images and descriptions were expanded or finished off with greater care. But the edition had also its defects. In substituting simple for inflated expressions, and in removing redundancies of description, the

poet occasionally rendered the passages bald and prosaic. His attempts
to generalize the technical details were also in some instances unfavourable.
Precision as well as animation was lost.   Mr. Clarke conceived that
Falconer, in his agitation and joy on being appointed to the *Aurora*, had
neglected this edition, and left the last alterations to his friend Mallet. This
is an unwarranted and, indeed, absurd conjecture, for Mallet had been four
years dead.   Whatever were the moral and mental defects of Mallet, he was
a good literary artist ; and had he retouched the Shipwreck, the poem, as
respects mere diction, would probably have been the better for his revision.
But Falconer's advertisement seems conclusive as to the third edition being
revised by himself; no other person would have taken such liberties with
his text, and the new passages introduced mark his own hand. He may,
however, have been hurried in his task by the necessity of preparing for
his departure ; and we think Mr. Clarke acted judiciously as editor of the
poem, in collating the different editions, and restoring the text to something
like distinctness and purity.   Not a line was inserted that had not been
sanctioned by the author—he was made to correct himself.   We have
followed Mr. Clarke's example in this reprint of the Shipwreck, but have
made a greater use of the third and latest edition—the last seen by the poet.

The *Aurora* sailed from Spithead on the 2nd of October 1769. Among
the passengers, besides the three commissioners, was the Rev. William
Hirst, chaplain to the expedition—an accomplished astronomer, who had
observed the transit of Venus, in 1761, at Madras, and who was afterwards
associated with the Astronomer Royal in Greenwich Observatory. From
a letter written by this gentleman we learn that the *Aurora* arrived at the
Cape of Good Hope on the 6th of December, that the commissioners had
been harmonious and happy on board ship, and had been hospitably received
by the Dutch governor and his council.   They made various excursions into
the country, and finally left the Cape, after a fortnight's stay, on the 27th
of December.   Captain Lee, who commanded the frigate, expressed his
intention of proceeding by the Mozambique Channel, instead of stretching
as usual into the great Indian Ocean, south of Madagascar.   There is now
little risk, by the diligent use of sextant and chronometer, in making this
passage during the fair season from April to September. But the Channel
abounds in shoals, and Captain Lee was a stranger to the navigation, while
the season was too far advanced.   The commissioners remonstrated, but
the captain was obstinate.   Mr. Vansittart was so impressed with the
danger of the rash experiment, that he would have quitted the *Aurora* if

another outward-bound East Indiaman had been then at the Cape. The *Aurora* sailed, and the result justified the worst fears that had been entertained—the ill-fated ship never reached its destination. Months and years elapsed, but no tidings came. The captain had spoken of touching at Johanna, one of the Comorro Islands, for provisions; he had also talked of landing on the island of St. Paul's; inquiries were made, but no trace of the vessel, after her leaving the Cape, was ever obtained. About four years afterwards, on the 19th of October 1773, a seaman, a negro, was examined before the East India Directors on the subject of the wreck. He stated that the *Aurora* had struck on a reef of rocks off Mocoa; that himself and four others were the only persons saved; that he and his companions had been two years on an island after their escape; and that they had at length been rescued by a country ship, which happened to touch at the island. What credit was given to the man's statement is not mentioned— the main fact, the loss of the *Aurora*, was, alas, but too apparent, and with her had perished the poet whose genius and fate have given so deep and melancholy an interest to the catastrophe.

> " Farewell, poor Falconer! When the dark sea
> Bursts like despair, I shall remember thee;
> Nor ever from the sounding beach depart
> Without thy music stealing on my heart,
> And thinking still I hear dread Ocean say,
> ' Thou hast declared my might, be thou my prey!'"
>   BOWLES.

The personal appearance and habits of Falconer have been minutely described by Mr. Clarke, from information communicated by those who knew the poet. "He was about five feet seven inches in height, with a dark weather-beaten complexion, and rather what is termed hard-featured, being considerably marked with the small-pox; his hair was of a brownish hue. In point of address his manner was blunt, awkward, and forbidding; but he spoke with great fluency; and his simple yet impressive diction was couched in words which reminded his hearers of the terseness of Swift. Though he possessed a warm and friendly disposition, he was fond of controversy, and inclined to satire. His observation was keen and rapid; his criticisms on any inaccuracy of language or expression were frequently severe; yet this severity was always intended to create mirth, and not by any means to show his superiority or to give the smallest offence. In his natural temper he was cheerful, and frequently used to amuse his messmates by composing acrostics on their favourites, in which he particularly excelled.

As a professional man, he was a thorough seaman; and, like most of that profession, was kind, generous, and benevolent." The last remark betrays the *amour propre* of the naval chaplain. Falconer himself was less laudatory of the mass of his brother sailors, and, like Fielding, when delineating their character, threw some shades into the picture.* He admitted, however, that there was to be found in almost every private sailor, a virtue which was unknown to many of his officers—the virtue of emulation. There was hardly a common tar, he said, who was not envious of superior skill in his fellows, and jealous on all occasions of being outdone in what he considered a branch of his duty. This was pre-eminently the case with our author himself. He not only mastered the principles and details of his profession, so as to be able to compile his elaborate Dictionary of the Marine, but he prided himself more on his reputation as a seaman than on his character as a poet.

The widow of Falconer (they had no children) long survived him. She obtained possession of his apartments in Somerset House, and was liberally assisted by Mr. T. Cadell, the publisher, who derived considerable profits from the continued sale of the Marine Dictionary and Shipwreck, of which he held the copyrights. Mr. Moser, already mentioned, in one of his numerous communications to the "European Magazine," states, that meeting the poet's widow one day, and expressing incidentally in conversation his admiration of the Shipwreck, she burst into tears. "She presented me," he adds, "with a copy of the Shipwreck, and seemed much affected by my commiseration of the misfortunes of a man whose work appears in its catastrophe prophetic." She died at Bath.

The fame of Falconer rests securely on this one monument of his genius. Though limited to the simplicity of a narrative of facts, and chiefly to a single incident, his poem of the Shipwreck possesses or suggests nearly all the primary elements of poetry and painting, of profound interest and over-

---

* See article "Midshipman" in his Marine Dictionary. "No character, in their opinion, is more excellent than that of the common sailor, whom they generally suppose to be treated with great severity by his officers......Blinded by these prepossessions, he (the midshipman) is thrown off his guard, and very soon surprised to find, amongst those honest sailors, a crew of abandoned miscreants, ripe for any mischief or villany. Perhaps, after a little observation, many of them will appear to him equally destitute of gratitude, shame, or justice, and only deterred from the commission of any crimes by the terror of severe punishment." Fielding, in his "Voyage to Lisbon," indulges in similar remarks. But it is scarcely necessary to add, that both the naval and military service have, by proper regulations and better instruction, been greatly elevated in moral character within the last century.

whelming pathos. The sea, with its various phenomena of beauty and terror, its storm and sunshine—the stately ship with its magnificent tracery and equipage, and its gallant crew—the classic and picturesque shores of the Mediterranean—and the appalling event of the shipwreck, with its horrors, despair, and death; such are the materials with which the poet had to deal in relating his story, "new to epic lore." The opening lines of the first canto strike the key-note, as it were, to a train of romantic and interesting associations :—

> " A ship from Egypt, o'er the deep impelled
> By guiding winds, her course for Venice held :
> Of famed Britannia were the gallant crew,
> And from that isle her name the vessel drew."

The name of *Britannia*, if fortuitous, was one of the felicities of the poet's subject; if assumed for the occasion, it furnishes an instance of his poetical art and skill. Had the ship been named the *Mary Jane*, or the *James Barnes*, the effect would have been very different. But still more important towards the poetical treatment of the subject was the scene of the catastrophe —the shores of Greece. All the images and recollections arising from beautiful scenery, the august remains of ancient art, and the wisdom and patriotism of the most heroic age of the world, were at once enlisted as auxiliaries of the story. The ship sailing along such shores became an object of deeper interest and of poetical sympathy; and its final destruction occurred at a spot memorable on that illustrious coast. "In all Attica," says Byron, "if we except Athens itself and Marathon, there is no scene more interesting than Cape Colonna. To the antiquary and artist, sixteen columns are an inexhaustible source of observation and design; to the philosopher, the supposed scene of Plato's conversations will not be unwelcome; and the traveller will be struck with the beauty of the prospect over 'isles that crown the Ægean deep;' but for an Englishman, Colonna has yet an additional interest, as the actual spot of Falconer's Shipwreck. Pallas and Plato are forgotten in the recollection of Falconer and Campbell :—

> ' Here in the dead of night, by Lonna's steep,
> The seaman's cry was heard along the deep.'"

This temple of Minerva may be seen at sea from a great distance; and the imagination instantly conjures up its appearance on that fatal day when the lightning flashed among the ruined columns, and the doomed vessel, driven like a fury by the storm, bounded through the waves towards the rocky shore. In the softer scenes of the poem this power of association and local painting has an inexpressible charm; and in the whole range of our descriptive poetry there is nothing finer than the pictures of the sunset and midnight on the shores of Candia, as seen from the sea. The solemn calm and delicious beauty and repose of this Eastern landscape prepare the reader, by contrast, for the nautical description that follows, which is brought out with great effect. The boatswain's whistle breaks the silence, and the order to weigh anchor is given. The sailors swarm aloft, fix the bars, and heave round the windlass :—

> " Up-torn reluctant from its oozy cave
> The ponderous anchor rises o'er the wave.
> High on the slippery masts the yards ascend,
> And far abroad the canvas wings extend.
> Along the glassy plain the vessel glides,
> While azure radiance trembles on her sides;
> The lunar rays in long reflection gleam,
> With silver deluging the fluid stream.
> Levant and Thracian gales alternate play,
> Then in the Egyptian quarter die away.
> A calm ensues: adjacent shores they dread,
> The boats, with rowers manned, are sent ahead;
> With cordage fastened to the lofty prow
> Aloof to sea the stately ship they tow;
> The nervous crew their sweeping oars extend,
> And pealing shouts the shore of Candia rend."

The ship is then minutely described. Falconer has been blamed for adding to it "frowning artillery;" but every Levant trader carried guns, and the *Britannia* is represented as a first-class merchantman. The natives gather round the shore in the noon-day sun to see the vessel depart "majestically slow before the breeze," the imperial flag unfurled :

> " Then towered the masts, the canvas swelled on high,
> And waving streamers floated in the sky.
> Thus the rich vessel moves in trim array,
> Like some fair virgin on her bridal day;
> Thus, like a swan, she cleaves the watery plain,
> The pride and wonder of the Ægean main."

It is impossible for word-painting to excel this in clear poetic beauty. Some of the smaller subsidiary sketches, as the waterspout, the dying dolphin, the troop of porpoises, &c., are also inimitable. The tragic portion of the poem is ushered in by a description remarkable for its vivid expression and melancholy grandeur:—

> " His race performed, the sacred lamp of day
> Now dipt in western clouds his parting ray :

> His languid fires, half lost in ambient haze,
> Refract along the dusk a crimson blaze ;
> Till deep immerged the sickening orb descends,
> And cheerless night o'er heaven her reign extends.
> Sad evening's hour, how different from the past!
> No flaming pomp, no blushing glories cast,
> No ray of friendly light is seen around ;
> The moon and stars in hopeless shade are drowned."

The characters of the chief officers of the vessel are well delineated and contrasted. Albert, the commander, is brave, liberal, and humane, "the father of his crew;" Rodmond, the next in command, is coarse, boisterous, and obstinate, yet dexterous and fearless as a seaman. One fine touch of humanity redeems his character : amidst the horrors of the wreck the helms-man is struck blind by the lightning—

> " Rodmond, who heard a piteous groan behind,
> Touched with compassion, gazed upon the blind ;
> And, while around his sad companions crowd,
> He guides the unhappy victim to the shroud:
> ' Hie thee aloft, my gallant friend !' he cries;
> ' Thy only succour on the mast relies.' "

The third in command is Arion, or Falconer himself, who is just men-tioned when this modest and striking transition is made :—

> " But what avails it to record a name
> That courts no rank among the sons of fame?"

Palemon, the friend of Arion, and his love story, somewhat interrupt the progress of the narrative, yet few readers would wish them away. His passion is one of unsophisticated nature and simple truth—a scene from Arcadian life—and it is in many parts touched with great delicacy and tenderness. Objection is more justly made to the historical episodes and classical allusions with which the poem abounds. These occur chiefly towards the close of the work, when the reader's anxiety and interest are strongly excited by the impending catastrophe. We see the ship "quivering o'er the topmost waves," or plunging headlong down the "horrid vale," the furious breakers lashing the strand on which the crew are every moment in danger of being dashed; and we are stopped with an enumeration of the ancient Grecian states and their philosophers, with the Delphic oracle, Par-nassus, and Helicon. There is much tawdry ornament, tumid expression, and forced comparison in these passages; but the poet no sooner touches the sea, than he regains his native strength. His verse rises and swells like the tempest, and in such lines as the following we hear the voice of a great poet mingling with the storm:—

> " Thus they direct the flying bark before
> The impelling floods, that lash her to the shore:
> High o'er the poop the audacious seas aspire,
> Uprolled in hills of fluctuating fire;
> With labouring throes she rolls on either side,
> And dips her gunnels in the yawning tide;
> Her joints, unhinged, in palsied languors play,
> As ice-flakes part beneath the noontide ray:
> The gale howls doleful through the blocks and shrouds,
> And big rain pours a deluge from the clouds;
> From wintry magazines that sweep the sky,
> Descending globes of hail impetuous fly;
> High on the masts, with pale and livid rays,
> Amid the gloom portentous meteors blaze:
> The ethereal dome, in mournful pomp arrayed,
> Now buried lies beneath impervious shade,
> Now, flashing round intolerable light,
> Redoubles all the horror of the night—
> Such terror Sinai's trembling hill o'erspread,
> When Heaven's loud trumpet sounded o'er its head:
> It seemed, the wrathful Angel of the wind
> Had all the horrors of the skies combined,
> And here, to one ill-fated ship opposed,
> At once the dreadful magazine disclosed."

And this angel of the wind is personified in a few lines of great power:—

> " And lo! tremendous o'er the deep he springs,
> The inflaming sulphur flashing from his wings:—
> Hark! his strong voice the dismal silence breaks,
> Mad Chaos from the chains of death awakes:
> Loud, and more loud, the rolling peals enlarge,
> And blue on deck the fiery tides discharge."

The resources of the seamen in this awful extremity, the throwing of the guns overboard, and the mournful consultation of the pilots, are depicted with a terrible reality. The incident of cutting down the mast seems like a great and sublime sacrifice, exciting intense sympathy:

> " Fast by the fated pine bold Rodmond stands,
> The impatient axe hung gleaming in his hands;
> Brandished on high, it fell with dreadful sound,
> The tall mast, groaning, felt the deadly wound;
> Deep gashed beneath, the tottering structure rings,
> And crashing, thundering, o'er the quarter swings."

The ship at length breaks up; we watch it with the painful interest due to a living being. Lifted high by a tremendous wave she strikes in her descent upon the marble crags, and, wounded, plunges and reels over the heaving surge; a second shock bilges the splitting vessel, and a third rends asunder the solid oak—

> " Her crashing ribs divide,
> She loosens, parts, and spreads in ruin o'er the tide."

The scene of agony and despair which ensues is portrayed with affecting minuteness and solemnity. No reckless or desperate seaman leaps overboard, anticipating death, as in the shipwreck described by Byron; there are no yells or demands for intoxicating drink; calm, manly sorrow and Christian resignation, mark the hour of horror and death. And when the tragedy has closed, the poet's art is seen in the picturesque addition of a troop of Grecian peasants, who, roused by the blustering tempest, repair to the summit of Cape Colonna, and gaze down with horror on the flood and ruin below. They descend to the beach to succour the few survivors—

> " Three still alive, benumbed and faint they find,
> In mournful silence on a rock reclined:
> The generous natives, moved with social pain,
> The feeble strangers in their arms sustain;
> With pitying sighs their hapless lot deplore,
> And lead them trembling from the fatal shore."

With these lines, so exquisite in their simplicity and pathos, the poem closes, like some magnificent and agitating piece of music, terminating in a few notes of plaintive melody.

Falconer composed his poem chiefly with a view to the gratification of his brother seamen, though they formed then, and form still, but a small proportion of his readers. He, therefore, made a liberal use of terms of art or technical expressions, the effect of which is to render some few passages obscure. They do not occur, however, in the more impassioned scenes, and their intrusion is amply compensated for by the air of truth and authenticity which they impart to the descriptions. We are taken on board the ship, as it were, instructed in its architecture, and witness every action of the crew. Attention is roused by the interjection of such phrases as *All hands unmoor! Reef topsails, reef!* or *Starboard again!* and their purport is soon ascertained. And all this professional lore of the poet is said to serve a purpose of practical utility and value. The poem, according to Mr. Clarke, " contains within itself the rudiments of navigation, if not to form a complete seaman, it may certainly be considered as the grammar of his professional science. I have heard (he adds) many experienced officers declare

3

that the rules and maxims delivered in this poem for the conduct of a ship in the most perilous emergency, form the best, indeed the only opinions which a skilful mariner should adopt. We possess, therefore, a poem not only eminent for its sublimity and pathos, but for an harmonious assemblage of technical terms and maxims used in navigation, which a young sailor may easily commit to memory; and also, with these, such scientific principles as will enable him to lay a sound foundation for his future professional skill and judgment." Poetry has seldom received or earned this praise of direct utility, for, though Virgil embodied in his exquisite verse the rules of husbandry, he never perhaps made a practical farmer. Nor would Falconer have taken his place as a British classic, if he had not soared far beyond his nautical precepts and description. These are only subordinate and accessory to his power of touching the heart and painting to the eye and imagination. In the light of his poetry the *Britannia* sails with a glory not its own, and the perils and adventures of the voyage are invested with a moral beauty and interest. It is this blending of the ideal with the real—of the picturesque and poetical with the pathetic and sublime—that constitutes the charm of the narrative; and a poem thus founded· on truth and nature, elevated by imagination, and presenting the most affecting examples of human suffering and moral heroism, may be said to rest on an imperishable basis. It has survived many revolutions of taste and opinion, and unquestionably will be read as long as British enterprise and valour maintain their empire on the sea.

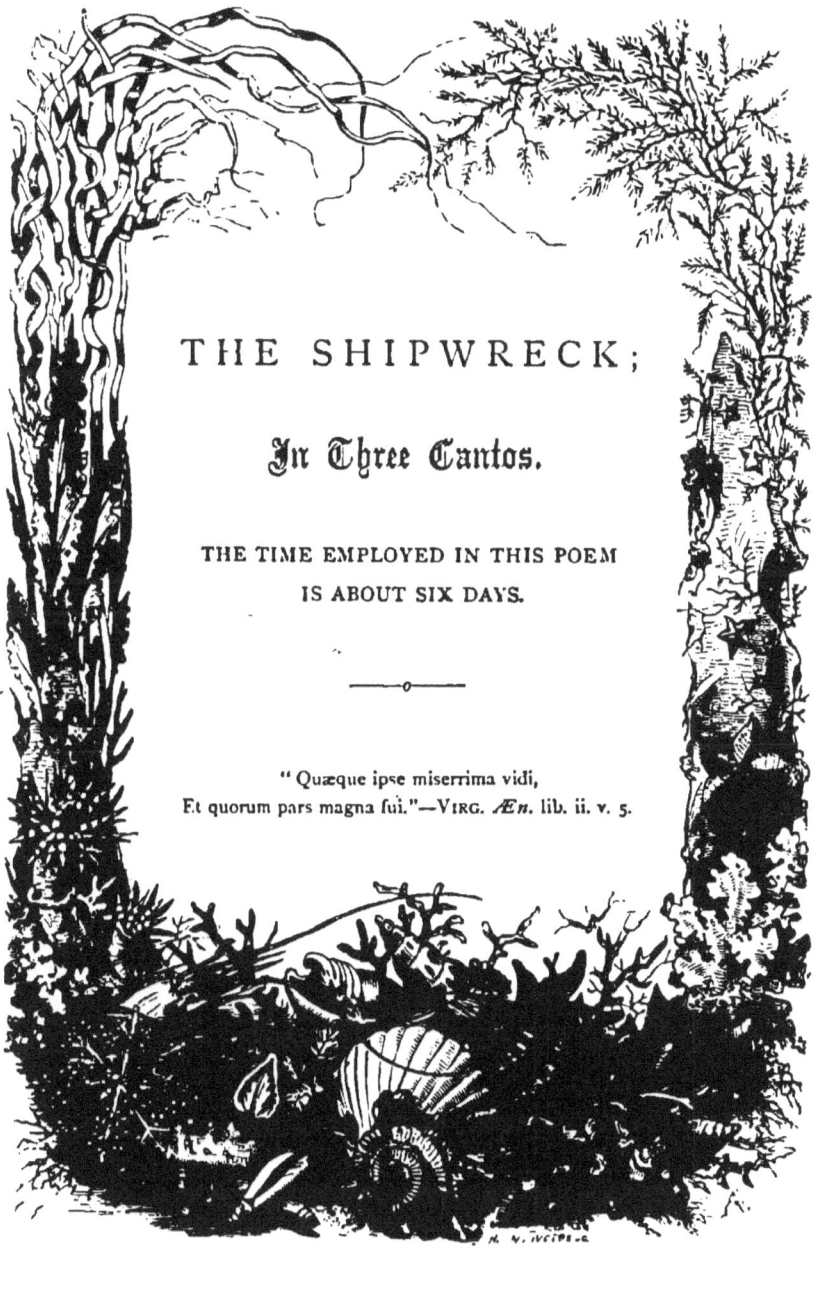

THE SHIPWRECK;

In Three Cantos.

THE TIME EMPLOYED IN THIS POEM
IS ABOUT SIX DAYS.

———o———

" Quæque ipse miserrima vidi,
Et quorum pars magna fui."—VIRG. Æn. lib. ii. v. 5.

INTRODUCTION.

WHILE jarring interests wake the world to arms,
And fright the peaceful vale with dire alarms;
While Albion bids the avenging thunders roll
Along her vassal deep from pole to pole ;
Sick of the scene, where War, with ruthless
    hand,
Spreads desolation o'er the bleeding land ;
Sick of the tumult, where the trumpet's breath
Bids ruin smile, and drowns the groan of death :

'Tis mine, retired beneath this cavern hoar,
That stands all lonely on the sea-beat shore,
Far other themes of deep distress to sing
Than ever trembled from the vocal string :
No pomp of battle swells the exalted strain,
Nor gleaming arms ring dreadful on the plain ;
But o'er the scene, while pale remembrance weeps,
Fate with fell triumph rides upon the deeps,
Where hostile elements conflicting rise,
And lawless surges swell against the skies,
Till hope expires, and peril and dismay
Wave their black ensigns on the watery way.
 Immortal train ! who guide the maze of song,
To whom all science, arts, and arms belong ;
Who bid the trumpet of eternal fame
Exalt the warrior's and the poet's name,
Or in lamenting elegies express
The varied pang of exquisite distress :
If e'er with trembling hope I fondly strayed,
In life's fair morn, beneath your hallowed shade,
To hear the sweetly-mournful lute complain,
And melt the heart with ecstasy of pain,
Or listen to the enchanting voice of love,
While all Elysium warbled through the grove ;
Oh ! by the hollow blast that moans around,
That sweeps the wild harp with a plaintive sound ;
By the long surge that foams through yonder cave,
Whose vaults remurmur to the roaring wave ;
With living colours give my verse to glow,
The sad memorial of a tale of woe !

A scene from dumb oblivion to restore,
To fame unknown, and new to epic lore !
  Alas ! neglected by the sacred Nine,
Their suppliant feels no genial ray divine :
Ah ! will they leave Pieria's happy shore
To plough the tide·where wintry tempests roar ?
Or shall a youth approach their hallowed fane,
Stranger to Phœbus and the tuneful train ?
Far from the Muses' academic grove
'Twas his the vast and trackless deep to rove ;
Alternate change of climates has he known,
And felt the fierce extremes of either zone :
Where polar skies congeal the eternal snow,
Or equinoctial suns for ever glow,
Smote by the freezing or the scorching blast,
" A ship-boy on the high and giddy mast," *
From regions where Peruvian billows roar,
To the bleak coasts of savage Labrador ;
From where Damascus, pride of Asian plains !
Stoops her proud neck beneath tyrannic chains,
To where the Isthmus,† laved by adverse tides,
Atlantic and Pacific seas divides.
But while he measured o'er the painful race
In fortune's wild illimitable chase,
Adversity, companion of his way,
Still o'er the victim hung with iron sway,
Bade new distresses every instant grow,
Marking each change of place with change of woe :

---

* Shakspeare's Henry IV., act iii.   † Darien.

In regions where the Almighty's chastening hand
With livid pestilence afflicts the land ;
Or where pale famine blasts the hopeful year,
Parent of want and misery severe ;
Or where, all-dreadful in the embattled line,
The hostile ships in flaming combat join ;
Where the torn vessel wind and wave assail,
Till o'er her crew distress and death prevail ;—
Such joyless toil in early youth endured,
The expanding dawn of mental day obscured,
Each genial passion of the soul oppressed,
And quenched the ardour kindling in his breast.
Then let not censure, with malignant joy,
The harvest of his humble hope destroy !
His verse no laurel wreath attempts to claim,
Nor sculptured brass to tell the poet's name.
If terms uncouth and jarring phrases wound
The softer sense with inharmonious sound,
Yet here let listening sympathy prevail,
While conscious Truth unfolds her piteous tale !
And lo ! the power that wakes the eventful song
Hastes hither from Lethean banks along :
She sweeps the gloom, and rushing on the sight,
Spreads o'er the kindling scene propitious light.
In her right hand an ample roll appears,
Fraught with long annals of preceding years,
With every wise and noble art of man,
Since first the circling hours their course began ;
Her left a silver wand on high displayed,
Whose magic touch dispels oblivion's shade.

Pensive her look ; on radiant wings that glow
Like Juno's birds, or Iris's flaming bow,
She sails ; and swifter than the course of light
Directs her rapid intellectual flight.
The fugitive ideas she restores,
And calls the wandering thought from Lethe's shores ;
To things long past a second date she gives,
And hoary time from her fresh youth receives ;
Congenial sister of immortal Fame,
She shares her power, and Memory is her name.
O first-born daughter of primeval time !
By whom transmitted down in every clime
The deeds of ages long elapsed are known,
And blazoned glories spread from zone to zone ;
Whose magic breath dispels the mental night,
And o'er the obscured idea pours the light ;
Say on what seas, for thou alone canst tell,
What dire mishap a fated ship befell,
Assailed by tempests, girt with hostile shores ?—
Arise ! approach ! unlock thy treasured stores !
Full on my soul the dreadful scene display,
And give its latent horrors to the day.

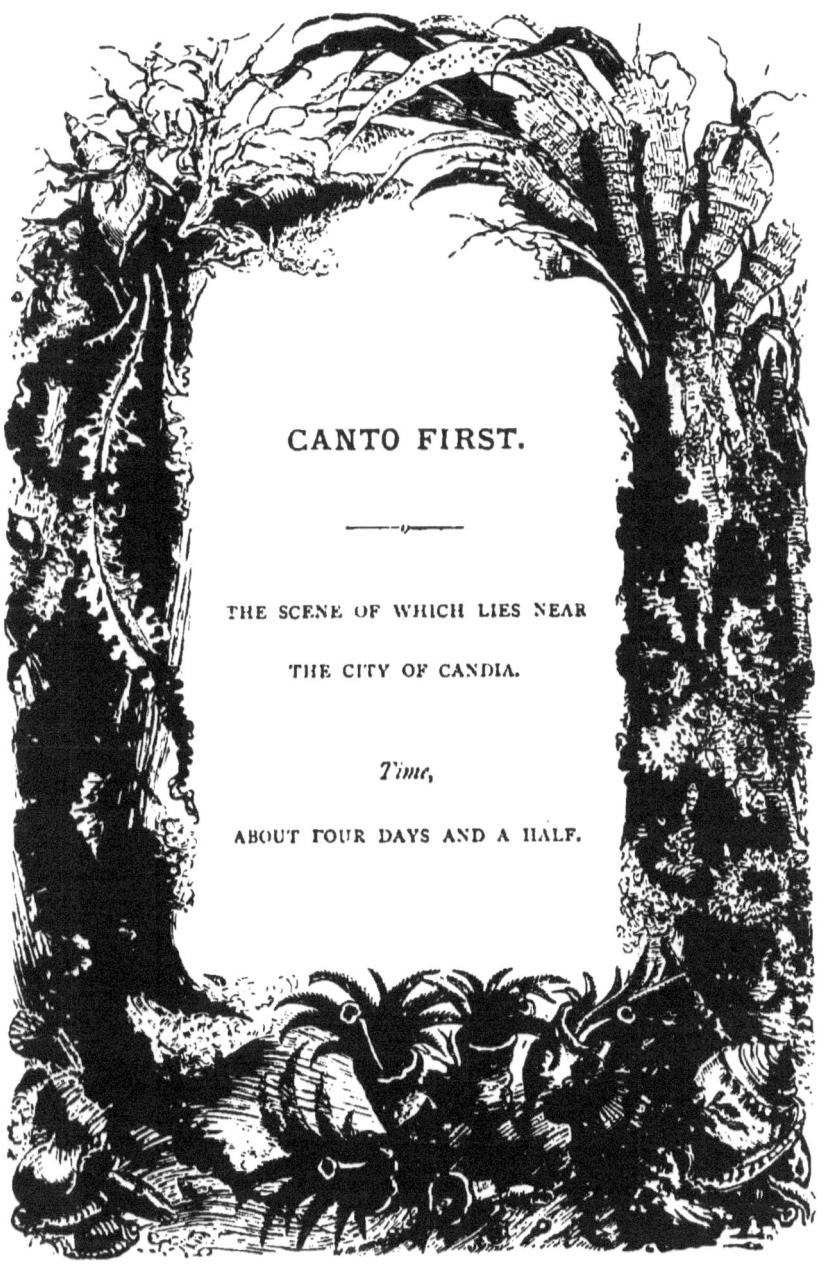

CANTO FIRST.

THE SCENE OF WHICH LIES NEAR

THE CITY OF CANDIA.

Time,

ABOUT FOUR DAYS AND A HALF.

THE ARGUMENT.

————o————

I. Retrospect of the Voyage—Arrival at Candia—State of that Island—Season of the Year described.—II. Character of the Master, and his Officers, Albert, Rodmond, and Arion—Palemon, Son to the Owner of the Ship—Attachment of Palemon to Anna, the Daughter of Albert—Noon.—III. Palemon's History.—IV. Sunset—Midnight—Arion's Dream—Unmoor by Moonlight—Morning—Sun's Azimuth taken—Beautiful Appearance of the Ship, as seen by the Natives from the Shore.

Canto First.

SHIP from Egypt, o'er the deep impelled
By guiding winds, her course for Venice held :
Of famed *Britannia* were the gallant crew,
And from that isle her name the vessel drew;
The wayward steps of Fortune, that delude
Full oft to ruin, eager they pursued ;
And, dazzled by her visionary glare,
Advanced incautious of each fatal snare,

Though warned full oft the slippery track to shun,
Yet Hope, with flattering voice, betrayed them on.
Beguiled to danger thus, they left behind
The scene of peace, and social joy resigned.
Long absent they from friends and native home
The cheerless ocean were inured to roam ;
Yet Heaven, in pity to severe distress,
Had crowned each painful voyage with success ;
Still, to compensate toils and hazards past,
Restored them to maternal plains at last.

Thrice had the sun, to rule the varying year,
Across the equator rolled his flaming sphere,
Since last the vessel spread.her ample sail
From Albion's coast, obsequious to the gale ;
She o'er the spacious flood, from shore to shore,
Unwearying wafted her commercial store ;
The richest ports of Afric she had viewed,
Thence to fair Italy her course pursued ;
Had left behind Trinacria's burning isle,
And visited the margin of the Nile :
And now, that winter deepens round the pole,
The circling voyage hastens to its goal :
They, blind to fate's inevitable law,
No dark event to blast their hope foresaw,
But from gay Venice, soon expect to steer
For Britain's coast, and dread no perils near ;
Inflamed by hope, their throbbing hearts elate,
Ideal pleasures vainly antedate :
Already British coasts appear to rise,
The chalky cliffs salute their longing eyes ;

Each to his breast, where floods of rapture roll,
Embracing strains the mistress of his soul;
Nor less o'erjoyed, with sympathetic truth,
Each faithful maid expects the approaching youth.
In distant souls congenial passions glow,
And mutual feelings mutual bliss bestow :
Such shadowy happiness their thoughts employ ;
Illusion all, and visionary joy !
    Thus time elapsed, while o'er the pathless tide
Their ship through Grecian seas the pilots guide.
Occasion called to touch at Candia's shore,
Which, blest with favouring winds, they soon ex-
    plore ;
The haven enter, borne before the gale,
Despatch their commerce, and prepare to sail.
    Eternal powers ! what ruins from afar
Mark the fell track of desolating war :

Here arts and commerce with auspicious reign
Once breathed sweet influence on the happy
    plain ;
While o'er the lawn, with dance and festive song,
Young Pleasure led the jocund hours along.
In gay luxuriance Ceres too was seen
To crown the valleys with eternal green :
For wealth, for valour, courted and revered,
What Albion is, fair Candia then appeared.—
Ah ! who the flight of ages can revoke ?
The free-born spirit of her sons is broke ;
They bow to Ottoman's imperious yoke.
No longer fame the drooping heart inspires,
For stern oppression quenched its genial fires :
Though still her fields, with golden harvests crowned,
Supply the barren shores of Greece around,
Sharp penury afflicts these wretched isles,
There hope ne'er dawns, and pleasure never smiles.
The vassal wretch contented drags his chain,
And hears his famished babes lament in vain.
These eyes have seen the dull reluctant soil
A seventh year mock the weary labourer's toil.
No blooming Venus, on the desert shore,
Now views with triumph captive gods adore ;
No lovely Helens now with fatal charms
Excite the avenging chiefs of Greece to arms ;
No fair Penelopes enchant the eye,
For whom contending kings were proud to die ;
Here sullen beauty sheds a twilight ray,
While sorrow bids her vernal bloom decay :

Those charms, so long renowned in classic strains,
Had dimly shone on Albion's happier plains!
Now in the southern hemisphere, the sun
Through the bright Virgin, and the Scales, had run,
And on the Ecliptic wheeled his winding way, ·
Till the fierce Scorpion felt his flaming ray.

Four days becalmed the vessel here remains,
And yet no hopes of aiding wind obtains;
For sickening vapours lull the air to sleep,
And not a breeze awakes the silent deep:
This, when the autumnal equinox is o'er,
And Phœbus in the north declines no more,
The watchful mariner, whom Heaven informs,
Oft deems the prelude of approaching storms.—
No dread of storms the master's soul restrain,
A captive fettered to the oar of gain:

His anxious heart, impatient of delay,
Expects the winds to sail from Candia's bay,
Determined, from whatever point they rise,
To trust his fortune to the seas and skies.

Thou living ray of intellectual fire,
Whose voluntary gleams my verse inspire,
Ere yet the deepening incidents prevail,
Till roused attention feel our plaintive tale,
Record whom chief among the gallant crew
The unblest pursuit of fortune hither drew :
Can sons of Neptune, generous, brave, and bold,
In pain and hazard toil for sordid gold ?—

They can ! for gold too oft with magic art
Can rule the passions and corrupt the heart :
This crowns the prosperous villain with applause,
To whom in vain sad merit pleads her cause ;
This strews with roses life's perplexing road,
And leads the way to pleasure's soft abode ;
This spreads with slaughtered heaps the bloody
plain,
And pours adventurous thousands o'er the main.

II. The stately ship, with all her daring band,
To skilful Albert owned the chief command :
Though trained in boisterous elements, his mind
Was yet by soft humanity refined;
Each joy of wedded love at home he knew,
Abroad, confest the father of his crew !
Brave, liberal, just ! the calm domestic scene
Had o'er his temper breathed a gay serene :

Him science taught by mystic lore to trace
The planets wheeling in eternal race;
To mark the ship in floating balance held,
By earth attracted, and by seas repelled ;
Or point her devious track through climes unknown
That leads to every shore and every zone.
He saw the moon through heaven's blue conclave glide,
And into motion charm the expanding tide,
While earth impetuous round her axle rolls,
Exalts her watery zone, and sinks the poles ;
Light and attraction, from their genial source,
He saw still wandering with diminished force ;
While on the margin of declining day
Night's shadowy cone reluctant melts away.
Inured to peril, with unconquered soul,
The chief beheld tempestuous oceans roll :
O'er the wild surge, when dismal shades preside,
His equal skill the lonely bark could guide ;
His genius, ever for the event prepared,
Rose with the storm, and all its dangers shared.

    Rodmond the next degree to Albert bore,
A hardy son of England's farthest shore,
Where bleak Northumbria pours her savage train
In sable squadrons o'er the northern main ;
That, with her pitchy entrails stored, resort
A sooty tribe to fair Augusta's port :
Where'er in ambush lurk the fatal sands,
They claim the danger, proud of skilful bands ;
For while with darkling course their vessels sweep
The winding shore, or plough the faithless deep,

O'er bar,* and shelf, the watery path they sound
With dexterous arm, sagacious of the ground :
Fearless they combat every hostile wind,
Wheeling in mazy tracks, with course inclined.
Expert to moor where terrors line the road,
Or win the anchor from its dark abode ;
But drooping, and relaxed, in climes afar,
Tumultuous and undisciplined in war.
Such Rodmond was ; by learning unrefined
That oft enlightens to corrupt the mind.
Boist'rous of manners ; trained in early youth
To scenes that shame the conscious cheek of truth ;
To scenes that nature's struggling voice control,
And freeze compassion rising in the soul :
Where the grim hell-hounds prowling round the shore
With foul intent the stranded bark explore ;
Deaf to the voice of woe, her decks they board,
While tardy justice slumbers o'er her sword.
The indignant Muse, severely taught to feel,
Shrinks from a theme she blushes to reveal.
Too oft example, armed with poisons fell,
Pollutes the shrine where Mercy loves to dwell :
Thus Rodmond, trained by this unhallowed crew,
The sacred social passions never knew.
Unskilled to argue, in dispute yet loud,
Bold without caution, without honours proud ;

---

* A *bar* is known, in hydrography, to be a mass of earth, or sand, that has been collected by the surge of the sea, at the entrance of a river or haven, so as to render navigation difficult and often dangerous. A *shelf,* or shelve, so called from the Saxon Schylf, is a name given to any dangerous shallows, sand banks, or rocks, lying immediately under the surface of the water.

In art unschooled, each veteran rule he prized,
And all improvement haughtily despised.
Yet, though full oft to future perils blind,
With skill superior glowed his daring mind,
Through snares of death the reeling bark to guide,
When midnight shades involve the raging tide.

To Rodmond next in order of command
Succeeds the youngest of our naval band :
But what avails it to record a name
That courts no rank among the sons of fame ;
Whose vital spring had just begun to bloom ˙
When o'er it sorrow spread her sickening gloom ?
While yet a stripling, oft with fond alarms
His bosom danced to nature's boundless charms ;
On him fair science dawned in happier hour,
Awakening into bloom young fancy's flower :
But frowning fortune with untimely blast
The blossom withered, and the dawn o'ercast.
Forlorn of heart, and by severe decree
Condemned reluctant to the faithless sea,
With long farewell he left the laurel grove
Where science and the tuneful sisters rove,
Hither he wandered, anxious to explore
Antiquities of nations now no more ;
To penetrate each distant realm unknown,
And range excursive o'er the untravelled zone.
In vain :—for rude Adversity's command
Still on the margin of each famous land,
With unrelenting ire his steps opposed,
And every gate of hope against him closed.

Permit my verse, ye blessed Pierian train !
To call Arion this ill-fated swain ;
For like that bard unhappy, on his head
Malignant stars their hostile influence shed.
Both in lamenting numbers, o'er the deep
With conscious anguish taught the harp to weep ;
And both the raging surge in safety bore
Amid destruction, panting to the shore.
This last, our tragic story from the wave
Of dark oblivion haply yet may save ;
With genuine sympathy may yet complain,
While sad remembrance bleeds at every vein.
    These, chief among the ships conducting train,
Her path explored along the deep domain ;
Trained to command, and range the swelling sail
Whose varying force conforms to every gale.
Charged with the commerce, hither also came
A gallant youth, Palemon was his name :
A father's stern resentment doomed to prove,
He came the victim of unhappy love !
His heart for Albert's beauteous daughter bled,
For her a sacred flame his bosom fed :
Nor let the wretched slaves of folly scorn
This genuine passion, Nature's eldest born !
'Twas his with lasting anguish to complain,
While blooming Anna mourned the cause in vain.
    Graceful of form, by nature taught to please,
Of power to melt the female breast with ease ;
To her Palemon told his tender tale,
Soft as the voice of Summer's evening gale :

His soul, where moral truth spontaneous grew,
No guilty wish, no cruel passion knew :

Though tremblingly alive to Nature's laws,
Yet ever firm to Honour's sacred cause ;
O'erjoyed, he saw her lovely eyes relent,
The blushing maiden smiled with sweet consent.

Oft in the mazes of a neighbouring grove
Unheard they breathed alternate vows of love :
By fond society their passion grew,
Like the young blossom fed with vernal dew ;
While their chaste souls possessed the pleasing pains
That Truth improves, and Virtue ne'er restrains.
In evil hour the officious tongue of Fame
Betrayed the secret of their mutual flame.
With grief and anger struggling in his breast
Palemon's father heard the tale confessed ;
Long had he listened with suspicion's ear,
And learnt, sagacious, this event to fear.
Too well, fair youth ! thy liberal heart he knew ;
A heart to nature's warm impressions true :
Full oft his wisdom strove with fruitless toil
With avarice to pollute that generous soil ;
That soil, impregnated with nobler seed,
Refused the culture of so rank a weed.
Elate with wealth in active commerce won,
And basking in the smile of fortune's sun ;
(For many freighted ships from shore to shore,
Their wealthy charge by his appointment bore ;)
With scorn the parent eyed the lowly shade
That veiled the beauties of this charming maid.
Indignant he rebuked the enamoured boy,
The flattering promise of his future joy ;
He soothed and menaced, anxious to reclaim
This hopeless passion, or divert its aim :
Oft led the youth where circling joys delight
The ravished sense, or beauty charms the sight.

With all her powers enchanting Music failed,
And Pleasure's siren voice no more prevailed.
Long with unequal art, in vain he strove
To quench the ethereal flame of ardent Love :
The merchant, kindling then with proud disdain,
In look, and voice, assumed a harsher strain.
In absence now his only hope remained ;
And such the stern decree his will ordained :
Deep anguish, while Palemon heard his doom,
Drew o'er his lovely face a saddening gloom ;
High beat his heart, fast flowed the unbidden
     tear,
His bosom heaved with agony severe ;
In vain with bitter sorrow he repined,
No tender pity touched that sordid mind—
To thee, brave Albert ! was the charge consigned.
The stately ship, forsaking England's shore,
To regions far remote Palemon bore.
Incapable of change, the unhappy youth
Still loved fair Anna with eternal truth ;
Still Anna's image swims before his sight
In fleeting vision through the restless night ;
From clime to clime an exile doomed to roam,
His heart still panted for its secret home.
     The moon had circled twice her wayward zone,
To him since young Arion first was known ;
Who wandering here through many a scene renowned,
In Alexandria's port the vessel found ;
Where, anxious to review his native shore,
He on the roaring wave embarked once more.

Oft by pale Cynthia's melancholy light
With him Palemon kept the watch of night,
In whose sad bosom many a sigh suppressed
Some painful secret of the soul confessed :
Perhaps Arion soon the cause divined,
Though shunning still to probe a wounded
      mind ;
He felt the chastity of silent woe,
Though glad the balm of comfort to bestow.
He, with Palemon, oft recounted o'er
The tales of hapless love in ancient lore,
Recalled to memory by the adjacent shore :
The scene thus present, and its story known,
The lover sighed for sorrows not his own.
Thus, though a recent date their friendship bore,
Soon the ripe metal owned the quickening ore;
For in one tide their passions seemed to roll, ·
By kindred age and sympathy of soul.

These o'er the inferior naval train preside,
The course determine, or the commerce guide:
O'er all the rest, an undistinguished crew,
Her wing of deepest shade Oblivion drew.

A sullen languor still the skies oppressed,
And held the unwilling ship in strong arrest:
High in his chariot glowed the lamp of day,
O'er Ida flaming with meridian ray,
Relaxed from toil, the sailors range the shore,
Where famine, war, and storm are felt no more;
The hour to social pleasure they resign,
And black remembrance drown in generous wine.

On deck, beneath the shading canvas spread,
Rodmond a rueful tale of wonders read,
Of dragons roaring on the enchanted coast;
The hideous goblin, and the yelling ghost:
But with Arion, from the sultry heat
Of noon, Palemon sought a cool retreat—
And lo! the shore with mournful prospects crowned,
The rampart torn with many a fatal wound,
The ruined bulwark tottering o'er the strand,
Bewail the stroke of war's tremendous hand:
What scenes of woe this hapless Isle o'erspread!
Where late thrice fifty thousand warriors bled.
Full twice twelve summers were yon towers assailed,
Till barbarous Ottoman at last prevailed;
While thundering mines the lovely plains o'erturned,
While heroes fell, and domes and temples burned.*

III. But now before them happier scenes arise,
Elysian vales salute their ravished eyes;
Olive and cedar formed a grateful shade,
Where light with gay romantic error strayed.
The myrtles here with fond caresses twine,
There, rich with nectar, melts the pregnant vine:
And lo! the stream renowned in classic song,
Sad Lethe, glides the silent vale along.
On mossy banks, beneath the citron grove,
The youthful wanderers found a wild alcove;

---

* These remarks allude to the ever-me-
morable Siege of Candia, which was taken
from the Venetians by the Turks in 1669;
being then considered as impregnable, and
esteemed the most formidable fortress in
the universe.

Soft o'er the fairy region languor stole,
And with sweet melancholy charmed the soul.
Here first Palemon, while his pensive mind
For consolation on his friend reclined,
In pity's bleeding bosom poured the stream
Of love's soft anguish, and of grief supreme—
" Too true thy words! by sweet remembrance taught,
My heart in secret bleéds with tender thought;
In vain it courts the solitary shade,
By every action, every look betrayed.
The pride of generous woe disdains appeal
To hearts that unrelenting frosts congeal:
Yet sure, if right Palemon can divine,
The sense of gentle pity dwells in thine.
Yes! all his cares thy sympathy shall know,
And prove the kind companion of his woe.
    " Albert thou know'st with skill and science graced;
In humble station though by fortune placed,
Yet never seaman more serenely brave
Led Britain's conquering squadrons o'er the wave:
Where full in view Augusta's spires are seen,
With flowery lawns and waving woods between,
A peaceful dwelling stands in modest pride,
Where Thames, slow winding, rolls his ample tide.
There live the hope and pleasure of his life,
A pious daughter, and a faithful wife.
For his return with fond officious care
Still every grateful object these prepare;
Whatever can allure the smell or sight,
Or wake the drooping spirits to delight.

" This blooming maid in Virtue's path to guide,
The admiring parents all their care applied;
Her spotless soul, to soft affection trained,
No vice untuned, no sickening folly stained :
Not fairer grows the lily of the vale
Whose bosom opens to the vernal gale:
Her eyes, unconscious of their fatal charms,
Thrilled every heart with exquisite alarms;
Her face, in beauty's sweet attraction dressed,
The smile of maiden innocence expressed;
While health, that rises with the new-born day,
Breathed o'er her cheek the softest blush of May:
Still in her look complacence smiled serene ;
She moved the charmer of the rural scene!
" 'Twas at that season when the fields resume
Their loveliest hues, arrayed in vernal bloom;

Yon ship, rich freighted from the Italian shore,
To Thames' fair banks her costly tribute bore:
While thus my father saw his ample hoard
From this return, with recent treasures stored;
Me, with affairs of commerce charged, he sent
To Albert's humble mansion—soon I went!
Too soon, alas! unconscious of the event.
There, struck with sweet surprise and silent awe,
The gentle mistress of my hopes I saw;
There, wounded first by Love's resistless arms,
My glowing bosom throbbed with strange alarms:
My ever charming Anna! who alone
Can all the frowns of cruel fate atone;
Oh! while all-conscious memory holds her power,
Can I forget that sweetly-painful hour
When from those eyes, with lovely lightning fraught,
My fluttering spirits first the infection caught?
When, as I gazed, my faltering tongue betrayed
The heart's quick tumults, or refused its aid;
While the dim light my ravished eyes forsook,
And every limb unstrung with terror shook.
With all her powers dissenting Reason strove
To tame at first the kindling flame of Love:
She strove in vain;—subdued by charms divine,
My soul a victim fell at beauty's shrine.
Oft from the din of bustling life I strayed,
In happier scenes to see my lovely maid;
Full oft, where Thames his wandering current
      leads,
We roved at evening hour through flowery meads;

There, while my heart's soft anguish I revealed,
To her with tender sighs my hope appealed :
While the sweet nymph my faithful tale believed,
Her snowy breast with secret tumult heaved ;
For, trained in rural scenes from earliest youth,
Nature was hers, and innocence, and truth.
She never knew the city damsel's art,
Whose frothy pertness charms the vacant heart—

My suit prevailed! for Love informed my tongue,
And on his votary's lips persuasion hung.
Her eyes with conscious sympathy withdrew,
And o'er her cheek the rosy current flew.
Thrice happy hours! where with no dark allay
Life's fairest sunshine gilds the vernal day:
For here the sigh that soft affection heaves,
From stings of sharper woe the soul relieves.
Elysian scenes! too happy long to last,
Too soon a storm the smiling dawn o'ercast;
Too soon some demon to my father bore
The tidings that his heart with anguish tore.
My pride to kindle, with dissuasive voice
Awhile he laboured to degrade my choice;
Then, in the whirling wave of Pleasure, sought
From its loved object to divert my thought.
With equal hope he might attempt to bind
In chains of adamant the lawless wind;
For Love had aimed the fatal shaft too sure,
Hope fed the wound, and Absence knew no cure.
With alienated look, each art he saw
Still baffled by superior Nature's law.
His anxious mind on various schemes revolved,
At last on cruel exile he resolved:
The rigorous doom was fixed; alas! how vain,
To him of tender anguish to complain.
His soul, that never love's sweet influence felt,
By social sympathy could never melt;
With stern command to Albert's charge he gave
To waft Palemon o'er the distant wave.

" The ship was laden and prepared to sail,
And only waited now the leading gale:
'Twas ours, in that sad period, first to prove
The heart-felt torments of despairing love;
The impatient wish that never feels repose,
Desire that with perpetual current flows,
The fluctuating pangs of hope and fear,
Joy distant still, and sorrow ever near.
Thus, while the pangs of thought severer grew,
The western breezes inauspicious blew,
Hastening the moment of our last adieu.
The vessel parted on the falling tide,
Yet time one sacred hour to love supplied:
The night was silent, and advancing fast,
The moon o'er Thames her silver mantle cast;
Impatient hope the midnight path explored,
And led me to the nymph my soul adored.
Soon her quick footsteps struck my listening ear,
She came confessed! the lovely maid drew near!
But, ah! what force of language can impart
The impetuous joy that glowed in either heart?
O ye! whose melting hearts are formed to prove
The trembling ecstasies of genuine love;
When with delicious agony, the thought
Is to the verge of high delirium wrought;
Your secret sympathy alone can tell
What raptures then the throbbing bosom swell;
O'er all the nerves what tender tumults roll,
While love with sweet enchantment melts the
   soul.

5

" In transport lost, by trembling hope impressed,
The blushing virgin sunk upon my breast,
While hers congenial beat with fond alarms;
Dissolving softness! paradise of charms!
Flashed from our eyes, in warm transfusion flew
Our blending spirits, that each other drew!
O bliss supreme! where Virtue's self can melt
With joys that guilty Pleasure never felt;
Formed to refine the thought with chaste desire,
And kindle sweet Affection's purest fire.
' Ah! wherefore should my hopeless love, (she cries,
While sorrow burst with interrupting sighs,)
For ever destined to lament in vain,
Such flattering, fond ideas entertain?
My heart, through scenes of fair illusion, strayed
To joys decreed for some superior maid.
'Tis mine abandoned to severe distress
Still to complain, and never hope redress—
Go then, dear youth! thy father's rage atone,
And let this tortured bosom beat alone.
The hovering anger yet thou may'st appease;
Go then, dear youth! nor tempt the faithless seas.
Find out some happier maid, whose equal charms,
With fortune's fairer joys, may bless thy arms:
Where, smiling o'er thee with indulgent ray,
Prosperity shall hail each new-born day:
Too well thou knowest good Albert's niggard fate
Ill fitted to sustain thy father's hate.
Go then, I charge thee by thy generous love,
That fatal to my father thus may prove;

On me alone let dark affliction fall,
Whose heart for thee will gladly suffer all.
Then haste thee hence, Palemon, ere too late,
Nor rashly hope to brave opposing fate.'
   " She ceased: while anguish in her angel-face
O'er all her beauties showered celestial grace:
Not Helen, in her bridal charms arrayed,
Was half so lovely as this gentle maid.
' O soul of all my wishes! (I replied)
Can that soft fabric stem affliction's tide?
Canst thou, fair emblem of exalted truth,
To sorrow doom the summer of thy youth;
And I, perfidious! all that sweetness see
Consigned to lasting misery for me?
Sooner this moment may the eternal doom
Palemon in the silent earth entomb;
Attest, thou moon, fair regent of the night!
Whose lustre sickens at this mournful sight:
By all the pangs divided lovers feel,
Which sweet possession only knows to heal;
By all the horrors brooding o'er the deep,
Where fate and ruin sad dominion keep;
Though tyrant duty o'er me threatening stands,
And claims obedience to her stern commands,
Should fortune cruel or auspicious prove,
Her smile, or frown, shall never change my love;
My heart, that now must every joy resign,
Incapable of change, is only thine.
   " ' Oh, cease to weep! this storm will yet decay,
And the sad clouds of sorrow melt away:

While through the rugged path of life we go,
All mortals taste the bitter draught of woe.
The famed and great, decreed to equal pain,
Full oft in splendid wretchedness complain:
For this, prosperity, with brighter ray,
In smiling contrast gilds our vital day.
Thou too, sweet maid! ere twice ten months are o'er,
Shalt hail Palemon to his native shore,
Where never interest shall divide us more.'——
   " Her struggling soul, o'erwhelmed with tender
       grief,
Now found an interval of short relief:
So melts the surface of the frozen stream
Beneath the wintry sun's departing beam.
With warning haste the shades of night withdrew,
And gave the signal of a sad adieu.
As on my neck the afflicted maiden hung,
A thousand racking doubts her spirit wrung:
She wept the terrors of the fearful wave,
Too oft, alas! the wandering lover's grave;
With soft persuasion I dispelled her fear,
And from her cheek beguiled the falling tear,
While dying fondness languished in her eyes
She poured her soul to Heaven in suppliant sighs:——
'Look down with pity, O ye powers above!
Who hear the sad complaint of bleeding love;
Ye, who the secret laws of fate explore,
Alone can tell if he returns no more :
Or if the hour of future joy remain
Long-wished atonement of long-suffered pain,

Bid every guardian-minister attend,
And from all ill the much-loved youth defend!'
With grief o'erwhelmed we parted twice in vain,
And, urged by strong attraction, met again.
At last, by cruel fortune torn apart,
While tender passion beat in either heart,
Our eyes transfixed with agonizing look,
One sad farewell, one last embrace we took.
Forlorn of hope the lovely maid I left,
Pensive and pale, of every joy bereft:

She to her silent couch retired to weep,
Whilst I embark'd, in sadness, on the deep."
    His tale thus closed, from sympathy of grief
Palemon's bosom felt a sweet relief:
To mutual friendship thus sincerely true,
No secret wish, or fear, their bosoms knew;

In mutual hazards oft severely tried,
Nor hope, nor danger, could their love divide.*

Ye tender maids! in whose pathetic souls
Compassion's sacred stream impetuous rolls,
Whose warm affections exquisitely feel
The secret wound you tremble to reveal;
Ah! may no wanderer of the stormy main
Pour through your breasts the soft delicious bane;
May never fatal tenderness approve
The fond effusions of their ardent love:

* This and the three preceding lines were deleted in the third edition, and the following (which seem worthy of preservation) substituted:—
" The hapless bird, thus ravished from the skies,
Where all forlorn his loved companion flies,
In secret long bewails his cruel fate,
With fond remembrance of his wingèd mate;
Till grown familiar with a foreign train,
Composed at length his sadly-warbling strain
In sweet oblivion charms the sense of pain."

Oh! warned by friendship's counsel, learn to
    shun
The fatal path where thousands are undone!
  Now, as the youths, returning o'er the plain,
Approached the lonely margin of the main,
First, with attention roused, Arion eyed
The graceful lover, formed in nature's pride:
His frame the happiest symmetry displayed,
And locks of waving gold his neck arrayed;
In every look the Paphian graces shine
Soft breathing o'er his cheek their bloom divine:
With lightened heart he smiled serenely gay,
Like young Adonis, or the son of May.
Not Cytherea from a fairer swain
Received her apple on the Trojan plain.

  IV. The sun's bright orb, declining all serene,
Now glanced obliquely o'er the woodland scene.
Creation smiles around; on every spray
The warbling birds exalt their evening lay:
Blithe skipping o'er yon hill, the fleecy train
Join the deep chorus of the lowing plain;
The golden lime and orange there were seen
On fragrant branches of perpetual green;
The crystal streams, that velvet meadows lave,
To the green ocean roll with chiding wave.
The glassy ocean hushed, forgets to roar,
But trembling murmurs on the sandy shore:
And lo! his surface lovely to behold
Glows in the west, a sea of living gold!

While, all above, a thousand liveries gay
The skies with pomp ineffable array. ―――――
Arabian sweets perfume the happy plains;
Above, beneath, around, enchantment reigns!
While glowing Vesper leads the starry train,
And Night slow draws her veil o'er land and main,
Emerging clouds the azure east invade,
And wrap the lucid spheres in gradual shade:

While yet the songsters of the vocal grove,
With dying numbers tune the soul to love :
With joyful eyes the attentive master sees
The auspicious omens of an eastern breeze.
Round the charged bowl the sailors form a ring;
By turns recount the wondrous tale, or sing,
As love, or battle, hardships of the main,
Or genial wine, awake the homely strain :
Then some the watch of night alternate keep,
The rest lie buried in oblivious sleep.

Deep midnight now involves the livid skies,
When eastern breezes from the shore arise :
The waning moon, behind a watery shroud,
Pale glimmered o'er the long-protracted cloud;
A mighty halo round her silver throne,
With parting meteors crossed, portentous shone :
This in the troubled sky full oft prevails,
Oft deemed a signal of tempestuous gales.

While young Arion sleeps, before his sight
Tumultuous swim the visions of the night:
Now blooming Anna with her happy swain
Approached the sacred hymeneal fane;
Anon, tremendous lightnings flash between,
And funeral pomp, and weeping loves are seen:
Now with Palemon, up a rocky steep,
Whose summit trembles o'er the roaring deep,
With painful step he climbed, while far above
Sweet Anna charmed them with the voice of Love;
Then sudden from the slippery height they fell,
While dreadful yawned beneath the jaws of hell—

Amid this fearful trance, a thundering sound
He hears, and thrice the hollow decks rebound;
Up starting from his couch on deck he sprung,
Thrice with shrill note the boatswain's whistle rung:
" All hands unmoor!" proclaims a boisterous cry,
" All hands unmoor!" the caverned rocks reply.
Roused from repose aloft the sailors swarm,
And with their levers soon the windlass* arm:
The order given, up springing with a bound
They fix the bars, and heave the windlass round,
At every turn the clanging pauls resound:
Up-torn reluctant from its oozy cave
The ponderous anchor rises o'er the wave.
High on the slippery masts the yards ascend,
And far abroad the canvas wings extend.
Along the glassy plain the vessel glides,
While azure radiance trembles on her sides;
The lunar rays in long reflection gleam,
With silver deluging the fluid stream.
Levant and Thracian gales alternate play,
Then in the Egyptian quarter die away.
A calm ensues: adjacent shores they dread,
The boats, with rowers manned, are sent ahead;
With cordage fastened to the lofty prow
Aloof to sea the stately ship they tow;†

---

* The *windlass* is a large roller, used to wind in the cable, or heave up the anchor. It is turned about by a number of long bars of levers, and is furnished with strong iron pauls to prevent it from recoiling. [*Paul*, a certain short bar of wood or iron fixed close to the capstern or windlass of a ship, to prevent those engines from rolling back or giving way when they are employed to heave in the cable or otherwise charged with any great effort.—*Falconer's Marine Dictionary.*]

† *Towing* is chiefly used as here, when a ship for want of wind is forced toward the shore, by the swell of the sea.

The nervous crew their sweeping oars extend,
And pealing shouts the shore of Candia rend:
Success attends their skill! the danger's o'er!
The port is doubled, and beheld no more.
   Now Morn with gradual pace advanced on high
Whitening with orient beam the twilight sky:
She comes not in refulgent pomp arrayed,
But frowning stern, and wrapt in sullen shade.
Above incumbent mists, tall Ida's* height,
Tremendous rock! emerges on the sight;
North-east, a league, the isle of Standia bears,
And westward, Freschin's woody cape† appears.
   In distant angles while the transient gales
Alternate blow, they trim the flagging sails;

---

* A mountain in the midst of Candia, or ancient Crete.

† Cape Freschin, or Frescia, is the eastermost part of two projecting points of land on the northern coast of Candia.

The drowsy air attentive to retain,
As from unnumbered points it sweeps the main.
Now swelling stud-sails* on each side extend,
Then stay-sails sidelong to the breeze ascend;
While all to court the veering winds are placed,
With yards alternate square, and sharply braced.

The dim horizon lowering vapours shroud,
And blot the sun yet struggling in the cloud;
Through the wide atmosphere condensed with haze,
His glaring orb emits a sanguine blaze,
The pilots now their azimuth† attend,
On which all courses, duly formed, depend:
The compass placed to catch the rising ray,
The quadrant's shadows studious they survey;
Along the arch the gradual index slides,
While Phœbus down the vertic-circle glides;
Now seen on ocean's utmost verge to swim,
He sweeps it vibrant with his nether limb.
Thus height and polar distance are obtained,
Then latitude, and declination, gained;
In chiliads next the analogy is sought,
And on the sinical triangle wrought:
By this magnetic variance is explored,
Just angles known, and polar truth restored.

The natives, while the ship departs their land,
Ashore with admiration gazing stand.

---

* *Stud*, or *studding-sails*, are light sails, which are extended in fine weather and fair winds beyond the skirts of the principal sails. *Stay-sails* are three-cornered sails, which are hoisted up on a strong rope called a Stay, when the wind crosses the ship's course either directly or obliquely.

† The operation of taking the sun's azimuth, in order to discover the eastern or western variation of the magnetical needle.

Majestically slow before the breeze
She moved triumphant o'er the yielding seas : *
Her bottom through translucent waters shone,
White as the clouds beneath the blaze of noon ;
The bending walest† their contrast next displayed,
All fore and aft in polished jet arrayed.

---

* In third edition :—" In silent pomp she marches on the seas."

† Before the art of coppering ships' bottoms was discovered, they were painted white. The *wales* are the strong flanks which extend along a ship's side, at different heights, throughout her whole length, and form the curves by which a vessel appears light and graceful on the water: they are usually distinguished into the main-wale and the channel-wale.

[In third edition the wales are graphically depicted :—

" The wales, that close above in contrast shone,

Clasp the long fabric with a jetty zone."]

BRITANNIA, riding awful on the prow,
Gazed o'er the vassal waves that rolled below :
Where'er she moved the vassal waves were seen
To yield obsequious, and confess their queen.
The imperial trident graced her dexter hand,
.Of power to rule the surge, like Moses' wand;
The eternal empire of the main to keep,
And guide her squadrons o'er the trembling deep :
Her left, propitious, bore a mystic shield,
Around whose margin rolls the watery field;
There her bold Genius, in his floating car,
O'er the wild billow hurls the storm of war :
And lo ! the beasts that oft with jealous rage
In bloody combat met, from age to age ;
Tamed into Union, yoked in friendship's chain,
Draw his proud chariot round the vanquished main :
From the proud margin to the centre grew
Shelves, rocks, and whirlpools, hideous to the view.
The immortal shield from Neptune she received,
When first her head above the waters heaved—
Loose floated o'er her limbs an azure vest,
A.figured scutcheon glittered on her breast ;
There from one parent soil, for ever young,
The blooming Rose and hardy Thistle sprung.
Around her head an oaken wreath was seen
Inwove with laurels of unfading green.
    Such was the sculptured prow ; from van to rear
The artillery frowned, a black tremendous tier!
Embalmed with orient gum, above the wave
The swelling sides a yellow radiance gave.

On the broad stern, a pencil warm and bold,
That never servile rules of art controlled,
An allegoric tale on high portrayed ;
There a young hero, here a royal maid:
Fair England's Genius in the youth expressed
Her ancient foe, but now her friend confessed,
The warlike nymph with fond regard surveyed ;
No more his hostile frown her heart dismayed :
His look, that once shot terror from afar,
Like young Alcides, or the god of war,
Serene as Summer's evening skies she saw ;
Serene, yet firm ; though mild, impressing awe :
Her nervous arm, inured to toils severe,
Brandished the unconquered Caledonian spear :
The dreadful falchion of the hills she wore,
Sung to the harp in many a tale of yore,
That oft her rivers dyed with hostile gore.
Blue was her rocky shield ; her piercing eye
Flashed like the meteors of her native sky ;
Her crest high-plumed, was rough with many a scar,*
And o'er her helmet gleamed the northern star.
The warrior youth appeared of noble frame,
The hardy offspring of some Runic dame :
Loose o'er his shoulders hung the slackened bow
Renowned in song, the terror of the foe !
The sword that oft the barbarous north defied,
The scourge of tyrants ! glittered by his side :

---

* [An echo of Pope's noble line :—
     " Old England's genius, rough with many a scar."]

Clad in refulgent arms in battle won,
The George emblazoned on his corselet shone ;
Fast by his side was seen a golden lyre
Pregnant with numbers of eternal fire :
Whose strings unlock the witches' midnight spell,
Or waft rapt Fancy through the gulfs of hell :
Struck with contagion, kindling Fancy hears
The songs of Heaven, the music of the spheres !
Borne on Newtonian wing through air she flies,
Where other suns to other systems rise.

These front the scene conspicuous ; overhead
Albion's proud oak his filial branches spread :
While on the sea-beat shore obsequious stood
Beneath their feet, the father of the flood :
Here, the bold native of her cliffs above,
Perched by the martial maid the bird of Jove ;
There, on the watch, sagacious of his prey,
With eyes of fire, an English mastiff lay :
Yonder fair Commerce stretched her wingèd sail,
Here frowned the god that wakes the living gale.
High o'er the poop, the flattering winds unfurled
The imperial flag that rules the watery world.
Deep blushing armours all the tops invest,
And warlike trophies either quarter dressed :
Then towered the masts, the canvas swelled on high,
And waving streamers floated in the sky.
Thus the rich vessel moves in trim array,
Like some fair virgin on her bridal day ;
Thus, like a swan, she cleaves the watery plain,
The pride and wonder of the Ægean main !

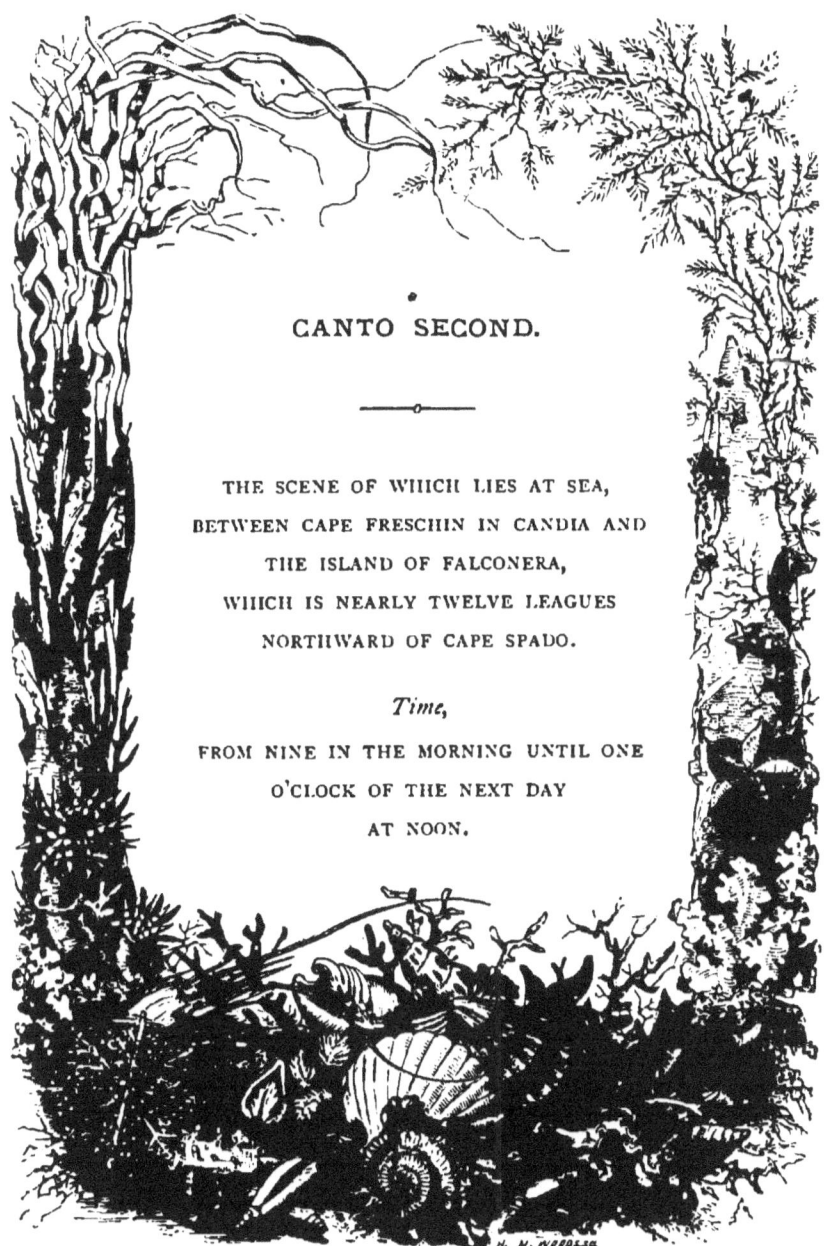

CANTO SECOND.

THE SCENE OF WHICH LIES AT SEA,
BETWEEN CAPE FRESCHIN IN CANDIA AND
THE ISLAND OF FALCONERA,
WHICH IS NEARLY TWELVE LEAGUES
NORTHWARD OF CAPE SPADO.

Time,

FROM NINE IN THE MORNING UNTIL ONE
O'CLOCK OF THE NEXT DAY
AT NOON.

6

THE ARGUMENT.

I. Reflections on leaving Shore.—II. Favourable Breeze—Waterspout—The Dying Dolphin—Breeze freshens—Ship's rapid Progress along the Coast—Top-sails Reefed—Gale of Wind—Last Appearance, Bearing, and Distance, of Cape Spado—A Squall—Top-Sails Double Reefed—Main-sail Split—The Ship Bears Away before the Wind; again Hauls upon the Wind—Another Main-sail Bent, and Set—Porpoises.—III. The Ship Driven Out of her Course from Candia—Heavy Gale—Top-sails Furled—Top-gallant-yards Lowered—Great Sea—Threatening Sunset—Difference of Opinion respecting the Mode of Taking in the Main-sail—Courses Reefed—Four Seamen Lost off the Lee Main-yard-arm—Anxiety of the Master and his Mates, on being near a Lee Shore—Mizzen Reefed.—IV. A Tremendous Sea bursts over the Deck; its Consequences—The Ship Labours in Great Distress—Guns Thrown Overboard—Dismal Appearance of the Weather —Very High and Dangerous Sea—Storm of Lightning—Severe Fatigue of the Crew at the Pumps—Critical Situation of the Ship near the Island Falconera—Consultation and Resolution of the Officers—Speech and Advice of Albert; his Devout Address to Heaven —Order Given to Bear Away—The Fore Stay-sail Hoisted and Split—The Head-yards Braced Aback—The Mizzen-mast Cut Away.

Canto Second.

ADIEU! ye pleasures of the sylvan scene,
   Where Peace and calm Contentment dwell
      serene :
   To me, in vain, on earth's prolific soil
   With summer crowned, the Elysian valleys smile ;
   To me those happier scenes no joy impart,
   But tantalize with hope my aching heart,
Ye tempests ! o'er my head congenial roll,
To suit the mournful music of my soul.—

In black progression, lo, they hover near,   .
Hail social horrors! like my fate severe :
Old Ocean hail! beneath whose azure zone
The secret deep lies unexplored, unknown.
Approach, ye brave companions of the sea!
And fearless view this awful scene with me.
Ye native guardians of your country's laws!
Ye brave assertors of her sacred cause!
The Muse invites you—judge if she depart
Unequal from the thorny rules of art.
In practice trained, and conscious of her power,
She boldly moves to meet the trying hour :
Her voice attempting themes, before unknown
To music, sings distresses all her own.

II. O'er the smooth bosom of the faithless
     tides,
Propelled by flattering gales, the vessel glides :
Rodmond exulting felt the auspicious wind,
And by a mystic charm its aim confined.
The thoughts of home that o'er his fancy roll,
With trembling joy dilate Palemon's soul ;
Hope lifts his heart, before whose vivid ray
Distress recedes, and danger melts away.
Tall Ida's summit now more distant grew,
And Jove's high hill was rising to the view ;
When on the larboard quarter they descry
A liquid column towering shoot on high ;
The foaming base the angry whirlwinds sweep,
Where curling billows rouse the fearful deep :

Still round and round the fluid vortex flies,
Diffusing briny vapours o'er the skies.
This vast phenomenon, whose lofty head
In Heaven immersed, embracing clouds o'erspread,
In spiral motion first, as seamen deem,
Swells, when the raging whirlwind sweeps the stream.
The swift volution, and the enormous train,
Let sages versed in Nature's lore explain—
The horrid apparition still draws nigh,
And white with foam the whirling billows fly.
The guns were primed; the vessel northward veers,
Till her black battery on the column bears :
The nitre fired ; and, while the dreadful sound
Convulsive shook the slumbering air around,
The watery volume trembling to the sky,
Burst down, a dreadful deluge from on high !
The expanding ocean trembled as it fell,
And felt with swift recoil her surges swell ;
But soon, this transient undulation o'er,
The sea subsides, the whirlwinds rage no more.
   While southward now the increasing breezes veer,
Dark clouds incumbent on their wings appear :
In front they view the consecrated grove
Of Cyprus, sacred once to Cretan Jove.
The thirsty canvas, all around supplied,
Still drinks unquenched the full aerial tide :
And now approaching near the lofty stern,
A shoal of sportive dolphins they discern
Beaming from burnished scales refulgent rays,
Till all the glowing ocean seems to blaze ;

In curling wreaths they wanton on the tide,
Now bound aloft, now downward swiftly glide ;
Awhile beneath the waves their tracks remain,
And burn in silver streams along the liquid plain.
Soon to the sport of death the crew repair,
Dart the long lance, or spread the baited snare.
One in redoubling mazes wheels along,
And glides unhappy near the triple prong :
Rodmond, unerring, o'er his head suspends
The barbed steel, and every turn attends ;
Unerring aimed, the missile weapon flew,
And, plunging, struck the fated victim through ;
The upturning points his pond'rous bulk sustain,
On deck he struggles with convulsive pain :
But while his heart the fatal javelin thrills,
And flitting life escapes in sanguine rills,
What radiant changes strike the astonished sight !
What glowing hues of mingled shade and light !
Not equal beauties gild the lucid west
With parting beams all o'er profusely dressed,
Not lovelier colours paint the vernal dawn
When orient dews impearl the enamelled lawn,
Than from his sides in bright suffusion flow,
That now with gold empyreal seem to glow ;
Now in pellucid sapphires meet the view,
And emulate the soft celestial hue ;
Now beam a flaming crimson on the eye,
And now assume the purple's deeper dye :
But here description clouds each shining ray,
What terms of Art can Nature's powers display ?

Now, while on high the freshening gale she feels,
The ship beneath her lofty pressure reels :
The lighter sails, for summer winds and seas,
Are now dismissed the straining masts to ease ;
Swift on the deck the stud-sails all descend,
Which ready seamen from the yards unbend ;
The boats then hoisted in, are fixed on board,
And on the deck with fastening gripes secured.
The watchful ruler of the helm, no more
With fixed attention eyes the adjacent shore,
But by the oracle of truth below,
The wondrous magnet, guides the wayward prow.
The powerful sails with steady breezes swelled,
Swift and more swift the yielding bark impelled :
Across her stem the parting waters run,
As clouds, by tempests wafted, pass the sun.
Impatient thus, she darts along the shore,
Till Ida's mount, and Jove's, are seen no more ;
And, while aloof from Retimo she steers,
Malacha's foreland full in front appears.
Wide o'er yon isthmus stands the cypress grove
That once inclosed the hallowed fane of Jove ;
Here, too, memorial of his name ! is found
A tomb in marble ruins on the ground :
This gloomy tyrant, whose despotic sway
Compelled the trembling nations to obey,
Through Greece for murder, rape, and incest known,
The Muses raised to high Olympus' throne ;
For oft, alas ! their venal strains adorn
The prince, whom blushing Virtue holds in scorn ;

Still Rome and Greece record his endless fame,
And hence yon mountain yet retains his name.

But see ! in confluence borne before the blast,
Clouds rolled on clouds the dusky noon o'ercast :
The blackening ocean curls, the winds arise,
And the dark scud* in swift succession flies.
While the swoln canvas bends the masts on high,
Low in the wave the leeward cannon † lie.
The master calls to give the ship relief,
" The top-sails ‡ lower, and form a single reef!"
Each lofty yard with slackened cordage reels ;
Rattle the creaking blocks and ringing wheels :
Down the tall masts the top-sails sink amain,
Are manned and reefed, then hoisted up again.
More distant grew receding Candia's shore,
And southward of the west Cape Spado bore.

Four hours the sun his high meridian throne
Had left, and o'er Atlantic regions shone ;——
Still blacker clouds, that all the skies invade,
Draw o'er his sullied orb a dismal shade.
A squall deep lowering blots the southern sky,
Before whose boisterous breath the waters fly ;

---

* The *scud* is a name given by seamen to the lowest and lightest clouds, which are swiftly driven along the atmosphere by the winds.

† When the wind crosses a ship's course, either directly or obliquely, that side of the ship upon which it acts is termed the *weather-side;* and the opposite one, which is then pressed downwards, is termed the *lee-side;* all on one side of her is accordingly called to windward, and all on the opposite side to leeward : hence also are derived the lee-cannon, the lee-braces, weather-braces, &c. The same term is used by Milton :—

" The pilot of some small night-foundered
   With fixed anchor,—   [skiff,
Moors by his side under the *lee.*"
                        Par. Lost, b. i. v. 204.

‡ The *top-sails* are large square sails of the second degree in height and magnitude. *Reefs* are certain divisions or spaces by which the principal sails are reduced when the wind increases ; and again enlarged proportionably when its force abates.

Its weight the top-sails can no more sustain—
" Reef top-sails, reef!" the master calls again.
The halyards* and top-bow-lines† soon are gone,
To clue-lines and reef-tackles‡ next they run :
The shivering sails descend ; the yards are square ;
Then quick aloft the ready crew repair :
The weather-earings,§ and the lee, they passed,
The reefs enrolled, and every point made fast.
Their task above thus finished, they descend,
And vigilant the approaching squall attend :
It comes resistless ! and with foaming sweep
Upturns the whitening surface of the deep ;
In such a tempest, borne to deeds of death,
The wayward sisters scour the blasted heath.
The clouds, with ruin pregnant, now impend,
And storm and cataract tumultuous blend.
Deep, on her side, the reeling vessel lies :
" Brail up the mizzen‖ quick !" the master cries,
" Man the clue-garnets !¶ let the main-sheet** fly !"
It rends in thousand shivering shreds on high !

---

* *Halyards* are those ropes by which sails are hoisted or lowered.

† *Bow-lines* are ropes fastened to the outer edge of square sails in three different places, that the windward edge of the sail may be bound tight forward on a side wind, in order to keep the sail from shivering.

‡ *Clue-lines* are fastened to the lower corners of the square sails, for the more easy furling of them. *Reef-tackles* are ropes fastened to the edge of the sail, just beneath the lowest reef ; and being brought down to the deck by means of two blocks, are used to facilitate the operation of reefing.

§ *Earings* are small ropes employed to fasten the upper corners of the principal sails, and the extremities of the reefs, to the respective yard-arms, particularly when any sail is to be close furled.

‖ The *mizzen* is a large sail of an oblong figure, extended upon the mizzen-mast.

¶ *Clue-garnets* are the same to the main-sail and fore-sail which the clue-lines are to all other square sails, and are hauled up when the sail is to be furled or brailed.

** *Sheets;* it is necessary in this place to remark that the sheets, which are universally mistaken by our English poets for the sails, are in reality the ropes that are used to extend the clues, or lower corners of the sails, to which they are attached.

The main-sail all in streaming ruins tore,
Loud fluttering, imitates the thunder's roar:
The ship still labours in the oppressive strain,
Low bending as if ne'er to rise again.
"Bear up the helm a-weather!"* Rodmond cries;
Swift at the word the helm a-weather flies;
She feels its guiding power, and veers apace,
And now the fore-sail right athwart they brace;
With equal sheets restrained, the bellying sail
Spreads a broad concave to the sweeping gale.
While o'er the foam the ship impetuous flies,
The helm the attentive timoneer† applies:

---

* The reason for putting the *helm a-weather*, or to the side next the wind, is to make the ship veer before it, when it blows so hard that she cannot bear her side to it any longer. *Veering*, or wearing, is the operation by which a ship, in changing her course from one board to the other, turns her stern to windward: the French term is, *virer vent arrière*.

† The helmsman, or steersman, from the French *timonnier*.

As in pursuit, along the aerial way,
With ardent eye the falcon marks his prey,
Each motion watches of the doubtful chase,
Obliquely wheeling through the liquid space ;
So, governed by the steersman's glowing hands,
The regent helm her motion still commands.
    But now, the transient squall to leeward past,
Again she rallies to the sullen blast :
The helm* to starboard moves ; each shivering sail
Is sharply trimmed to clasp the augmenting gale—
The mizzen draws ; she springs aloof once more,
While the fore stay-sail† balances before.
The fore-sail braced obliquely to the wind,
They near the prow the extended tack‡ confined :
Then on the leeward sheet the seamen bend,
And haul the bow-line to the bowsprit-end.
To top-sails next they haste : the bunt-lines§ gone !
Through rattling blocks the clue-lines swiftly run ;
The extending sheets on either side are manned,
Abroad they come ! the fluttering sails expand ;

---

* The helm, being turned to starboard, or to the right side of the ship, directs the prow to the left, or to port, and *vice versa.* Hence the helm being put a *starboard,* when the ship is running northward, directs her prow towards the west.

† Called with more propriety the *fore top-mast stay-sail:* it is of a triangular shape, and runs upon the fore top-mast stay, over the bowsprit ; it consequently has an influence on the fore part of the ship, as the mizzen has on the hinder part ; and, when thus used together, they may be said to balance each other. (See also the last note of this Canto.)

‡ The main-sail and fore-sail of a ship are furnished with a tack on each side, which is formed of a thick rope tapering to the end, having a knot wrought upon the largest extremity, by which it is firmly retained in the clue of the sail : by this means the tack is always fastened to windward, at the same time that the sheet extends the sail to leeward.

§ *Bunt-lines* are ropes fastened to the bottoms of the square sails, to draw them up to the yards, when the sails are brailed or furled.

The yards again ascend each comrade mast,
The leeches taught the halyards are made fast,
The bow-lines hauled, and yards to starboard braced,*
And straggling ropes in pendent order placed.
The main-sail, by the squall so lately rent,
In streaming pendants flying, is unbent :
With brails† refixed, another soon prepared,
Ascending, spreads along beneath the yard.
To each yard-arm the head-rope‡ they extend,
And soon their earings and their robans§ bend.
That task performed, they first the braces‖ slack,
Then to the chesstree drag the unwilling tack :
And, while the lee clue-garnet's lowered away,
Taught aft the sheet they tally and belay.¶
Now to the north, from Afric's burning shore,
A troop of porpoises their course explore ;
In curling wreaths they gambol on the tide,
Now bound aloft, now down the billow glide :

---

* A *yard* is said to be *braced* when it is turned about the most horizontally, either to the right or left : the ropes employed in this service are accordingly called *braces*.

† *Brails:* a general name given to all the ropes which are employed to haul up or brail the bottoms and lower corners of the great sails.

‡ A rope is always attached to the edges of the sails, to strengthen, and prevent them from rending : those parts of it which are on the perpendicular or sloping edges are called *leech-ropes;* that at the bottom, the *foot-rope ;* and that on the top, or upper edge, the *head-rope.*

§ *Robans,* or rope-bands, are small pieces of rope, of a sufficient length to pass two or three times about the yards, in order to fix to them the upper edges of the respective great sails : the robans, for this purpose, are passed through the eyelet-holes under the head-rope.

‖ Because the lee-brace confines the yard, so that the tack will not come down to its place till the braces are cast loose. [Chess-trees, mentioned in the next line, are thus explained by Falconer in his Dictionary : "Two pieces of wood bolted perpendicularly, one on the starboard and the other on the larboard side of the ship. They are used to confine the *clue* or lower corners of the mainsail ; for which purpose there is a hole in the upper part, through which the rope passes, that usually extends the clue of the sail to windward."]

¶ *Taught* implies stiff, tense, or extended straight ; and *tally* is a phrase particularly applied to the operation of hauling aft the sheets, or drawing them towards the ship's stern. To *belay,* is to fasten.

Their tracks awhile the hoary waves retain,
That burn in sparkling trails along the main—
These fleetest coursers of the finny race,
When threatening clouds the ethereal vault deface,
Their route to leeward still sagacious form,
To shun the fury of the approaching storm.

    III. Fair Candia now no more beneath her
        lee
Protects the vessel from the insulting sea ;
Round her broad arms, impatient of control,
Roused from the secret deep, the billows roll :
Sunk were the bulwarks of the friendly shore,
And all the scene a hostile aspect wore.
The flattering wind, that late with promised aid
From Candia's bay the unwilling ship betrayed,
No longer fawns beneath the fair disguise,
But like a ruffian on his quarry flies :
Tossed on the tide, she feels the tempest blow,
And dreads the vengeance of so fell a foe—
As the proud horse, with costly trappings gay,
Exulting, prances to the bloody fray ;
Spurning the ground, he glories in his might,
But reels tumultuous in the shock of fight :
Ev'n so, caparisoned in gaudy pride,
The bounding vessel dances on the tide.

    Fierce and more fierce the gathering tempest grew,
South, and by west, the threatening demon blew :
The ship no longer can her top-sails spread,
And every hope of fairer skies is fled.

Bow-lines and halyards are cast off again,
Clue-lines hauled down, and sheets let fly amain :
Embrailed each top-sail, and by braces squared,
The seamen climb aloft and man each yard :
They furled the sails, and pointed to the wind
The yards, by rolling tackles* then confined,
While o'er the ship the gallant boatswain flies ;
Like a hoarse mastiff through the storm he cries.
Prompt to direct the unskilful still appears,
The expert he praises, and the timid cheers.
Now some, to strike top-gallant-yards† attend,
Some, travellers‡ up the weather-back-stays send,
At each mast-head the top-ropes§ others bend.
The parrels,|| lifts,¶ and clue-lines soon are gone,
Topped and unrigged they down the back-stays run ;
The yards secure along the booms** were laid,
And all the flying ropes aloft belayed.

---

* The *rolling-tackle* is an assemblage of pulleys, used to confine the yard to the weather-side of the mast, and prevent the former from rubbing against the latter by the fluctuating motion of the ship in a turbulent sea.

† *Top-gallant-yards*, which are the highest ones in a ship, are sent down at the approach of a heavy gale, to ease the mast-heads.

‡ *Travellers* are iron rings furnished with a piece of rope, one end of which encircles the ring to which it is spliced : they are principally intended to facilitate the hoisting or bowering of the top-gallant-yards ; for which purpose two of them are fixed on each *back-stay;* which are long ropes that reach, on each side the ship, from the top-masts (which are the second in point of height) to the chains.

§ *Top-ropes* are employed to sway up or lower the top-masts, top-gallant-masts, and their respective yards.

|| *Parrels* are those bands of rope by which the yards are fastened to the masts, so as to slide up and down when requisite : and of these there are four different sorts.

¶ *Lifts* are ropes which reach from each mast-head to their respective yard-arms. A yard is said to be *topped* when one end of the yard is raised higher than the other, in order to lower it on deck by means of the top-ropes.

** *Booms* are spare masts, or yards, which are placed in store on deck, between the main and fore-mast, immediately to supply the place of any that may be carried away or injured by stress of weather.

Their sails reduced, and all the rigging clear,
Awhile the crew relax from toils severe ;
Awhile, their spirits with fatigue oppressed,
In vain expect the alternate hour of rest—
But with redoubling force the tempests blow,
And watery hills in dread succession flow :

A dismal shade o'ercasts the frowning skies,
New troubles grow, new difficulties rise ;
No season this from duty to descend !—
" All hands on deck " must now the storm attend.
His race performed, the sacred lamp of day
Now dipt in western clouds his parting ray :

His languid fires, half lost in ambient haze,
Refract along the dusk a crimson blaze ;
Till deep immerged the sickening orb descends,
And cheerless Night o'er Heaven her reign extends.
Sad evening's hour, how different from the past !
No flaming pomp, no blushing glories cast,
No ray of friendly light is seen around ;
The moon and stars in hopeless shade are drowned.
The ship no longer can her courses* bear,
To reef them now becomes the master's care ;
The sailors summoned aft, all ready stand,
And man the enfolding brails at his command :
But here the doubtful officers dispute,†
Till skill and judgment prejudice confute :
For Rodmond to new methods still a foe,
Would first, at all events, the sheet let go ;
To long-tried practice obstinately warm,
He doubts conviction, and relies on form.
This Albert and Arion disapprove,
And first to brail the tack up firmly move :—
" The watchful seaman, whose sagacious eye
On sure experience may with truth rely,

---

* The *courses* are generally understood to be the main-sail, fore-sail, and mizzen, which are the largest and lowest sails on their several masts; the term is, however, sometimes taken in a larger sense.

This is particularly mentioned, not because there was, or could be, any dispute at such a time between the master of a ship and his chief mate, as the former can always command the latter, but to expose the obstinacy of a number of our veteran officers, who would rather risk anything than forego their ancient rules, although many of them are in the highest degree equally absurd and dangerous. It is to the wonderful sagacity of these philosophers that we owe the sea-maxims of avoiding to whistle in a storm, because it will increase the wind ; of whistling on the wind in a calm ; of nailing horse-shoes on the mast, to prevent the power of witches ; of nailing a fair wind to the starboard cat-head, &c.

Who from the reigning cause foretels the effect,
This barbarous practice ever will reject;
For, fluttering loose in air, the rigid sail
Soon flits to ruins in the furious gale;
And he, who strives the tempest to disarm,
Will never first embrail the lee yard-arm."
So Albert spoke; to windward, at his call,
Some seamen the clue-garnet stand to haul—
The tack's * eased off; while the involving clue
Between the pendent blocks ascending flew;
The sheet and weather-brace † they now stand by,
The lee clue-garnet, and the bunt-lines ply:
Then, all prepared, " Let go the sheet !" he cries—
Loud rattling, jarring, through the blocks it flies !
Shivering at first, till by the blast impelled
High o'er the lee yard-arm the canvas swelled;
By spilling-lines ‡ embraced, with brails confined,
It lies at length unshaken by the wind.
The fore-sail then secured with equal care,
Again to reef the main-sail they repair;
While some above the yard o'er-haul the tye,
Below, the down-haul tackle § others ply,

---

* It has been already remarked, that the *tack* is always fastened to windward; consequently, as soon as it is cast loose, and the clue-garnet is hauled up, the weather clue of the sail immediately mounts to the yard; and this operation must be carefully performed in a storm, to prevent the sail from splitting, or being torn to pieces by shivering.

† Whenever the *sheet* is cast off, it is necessary to pull in the *weather-brace*, to prevent the violent shaking of the sail.

‡ The *spilling-lines*, which are only used on particular occasions in tempestuous weather, are employed to draw together, and confine the belly of the sail, when inflated by the wind over the yard.

§ The violence of the gale forcing the yard much out, it could not easily have been lowered so as to reef the sail, without the application of a *tackle*, consisting of an assemblage of pulleys, to haul it down on the mast: this is afterwards converted into rolling tackle, which has been already described in a note, p. 94.

7

Jears,* lifts, and brails, a seaman each attends,
And down the mast its mighty yard descends:
When lowered sufficient they securely brace,
And fix the rolling tackle in its place;
The reef-lines † and their earings now prepared,
Mounting on pliant shrouds,‡ they man the yard;
Far on the extremes appear two able hands,
For no inferior skill this task demands—
To windward, foremost, young Arion strides,
The lee yard-arm the gallant boatswain rides:
Each earing to its cringle first they bend,
The reef-band § then along the yard extends;
The circling earing round the extremes entwined,
By outer and by inner turns ‖ they bind;
The reef-lines next from hand to hand received,
Through eyelet-holes and roban-legs were reeved;
The folding reefs in plaits enrolled they lay,
Extend the worming lines, and ends belay.

  Hadst thou, Arion ! held the leeward post
While on the yard by mountain billows tossed,
Perhaps Oblivion o'er our tragic tale
Had then for ever drawn her dusky veil;

---

* *Jears*, or geers, answer the same purpose to the main-sail, fore-sail, and mizzen, as halyards do to all inferior sails. The *bye*, a sort of runner, or thick rope, is the upper part of the jears.

† *Reef-lines* are only used to reef the main-sail and fore-sail.

‡ *Shrouds*, so called from the Saxon Scrud, consist of a range of thick ropes stretching downwards from the mast-heads to the right and left sides of a ship, in order to support the masts, and enable them to carry sail; they are also used as rope-ladders, by which seamen ascend, or descend, to execute whatever is wanting to be done about the sails and rigging.

§ *Reef-band* consists of a piece of canvas sewed across the sail, to strengthen it in the place where the eyelet-holes of the reefs are formed.

‖ The *outer turns* of the earing serve to extend the sail along its yard; the *inner turns* are employed to confine its head-rope close to its surface.

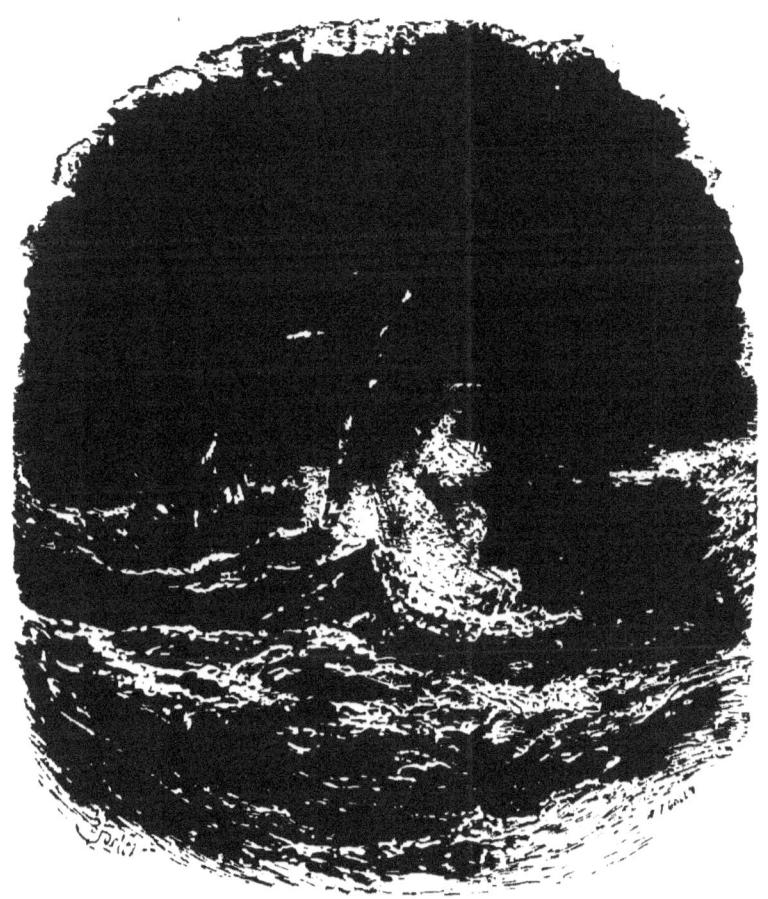

But ruling Heaven prolonged thy vital date,
Severer ills to suffer and relate.
    For, while aloft the order those attend
To furl the main-sail, or on deck descend;
A sea,* up-surging with stupendous roll,
To instant ruin seems to doom the whole:

---

* *A sea* is the general term given by | when such a wave bursts over the deck, the
sailors to an enormous wave; and hence, | vessel is said to have shipped a sea.

"O friends, secure your hold!" Arion cries—
It comes all dreadful! down the vessel lies
Half buried sideways; while, beneath it tossed,
Four seamen off the lee yard-arm are lost:
Torn with resistless fury from their hold,
In vain their struggling arms the yard enfold ;
In vain to grapple flying ropes they try,
The ropes, alas! a solid gripe deny:
Prone on the midnight surge with panting breath
They cry for aid, and long contend with death ;
High o'er their heads the rolling billows sweep,
And down they sink in everlasting sleep—
Bereft of power to help, their comrades see
The wretched victims die beneath the lee,
With fruitless sorrow their lost state bemoan,
Perhaps, a fatal prelude to their own !
    In dark suspense on deck the pilots stand,
Nor can determine on the next command :
Though still they knew the vessel's armed side
Impenetrable to the clasping tide;
Though still the waters by no secret wound
A passage to her deep recesses found;
Surrounding evils yet they ponder o'er,
A storm, a dangerous sea, and leeward shore !
"Should they, though reefed, again their sails ex-
        tend,
Again in shivering streamers they may rend;
Or, should they stand, beneath the oppressive
        strain
The down-pressed ship may never rise again;

Too late to weather * now Morea's land,

And drifting fast on Athen's rocky strand "—

Thus they lament the consequence severe,

Where perils unallayed by hope appear:

Long pondering in their minds each feared event,

At last to furl the courses they consent;

That done, to reef the mizzen next agree,

And try † beneath it sidelong in the sea.

Now down the mast the yard they lower away,

Then jears and topping-lift ‡ secure belay;

The head, with doubling canvas fenced around,

In balance near the lofty peak they bound;

The reef enwrapped, the inserted knittles tied,

The halyards throat and peak are next applied—

The order given, the yard aloft they swayed,

The brails relaxed, the extended sheet belayed;

The helm its post forsook, and, lashed a-lee, §

Inclined the wayward prow to front the sea.

IV. When sacred Orpheus on the Stygian coast,

 ` With notes divine deplored his consort lost;

---

* To *weather a shore* is to pass to windward of it, which at this time was prevented by the violence of the gale. *Drift* is that motion and direction, by which a vessel is forced to leeward sideways, when she is unable any longer to carry sail; or, at least, is restrained to such a portion of sail, as may be necessary to keep her sufficiently inclined to one side, that she may not be dismasted by her violent labouring produced by the turbulence of the sea.

† To *try*, is to lay the ship with her side nearly in the direction of the wind and sea, with her head somewhat inclined to windward; the helm being fastened close to the lee-side, or, ih the sea language, hard a-lee, to retain her in that position. (See a further illustration in the last note of this Canto.)

‡ A tackle, or assemblage of pulleys, which *tops* the upper end of the mizzen-yard. This line, and the six following, describe the operation of reefing and balancing the mizzen. The *knittle* is a short line used to reef the sails by the bottom. The *throat* is that part of the mizzen-yard which is close to the mast.

§ *Lashed a-lee*, is fastened to the lee-side. See note, p. 88.

Though round him perils grew in fell array,
And fates and furies stood to bar his way;
Not more adventurous was the attempt to move
The infernal powers with strains of heavenly love,
Than mine to bid the unwilling Muse explore
The wilderness of rude mechanic lore :
Such arduous toil sage Dædalus endured
In mazes, self-invented, long immured,
Till Genius her superior aid bestowed,
To guide him through that intricate abode—
Thus long imprisoned in a rugged way
Where Phœbus' daughters never aimed to stray,
The Muse, that tuned to barbarous sounds her string,
Now spreads, like Dædalus, a bolder wing;
The verse begins in softer strains to flow,
Replete with sad variety of woe.

As yet, amid this elemental war,
Where Desolation in his gloomy car
Triumphant rages round the starless void,
And Fate on every billow seems to ride;
Nor toil, nor hazard, nor distress appear
To sink the seamen with unmanly fear :
Though their firm hearts no pageant-honour boast,
They scorn the wretch that trembles at his post;
Who from the face of danger strives to turn,
Indignant from the social hour they spurn :
Though now full oft they felt the raging tide
In proud rebellion climb the vessel's side;
Though every rising wave more dreadful grows,
And in succession dire the deck o'erflows,

No future ills unknown their souls appal,
They know no danger, or they scorn it all !
But even the generous spirits of the brave,
Subdued by toil, a friendly respite crave;
A short repose alone their thoughts implore,
Their harassed powers by slumber to restore.

    Far other cares the master's mind employ,
Approaching perils all his hopes destroy:
In vain he spreads the graduated chart,
And bounds the distance by the rules of art;
Across the geometric plane expands
The compasses to circumjacent lands;
.Ungrateful task ! for, no asylum found,
Death yawns on every leeward shore around—
While Albert thus, with horrid doubts dismayed,
The geometric distances surveyed;
On deck the watchful Rodmond cries aloud,
"Secure your lives ! grasp every man a shroud "—
Roused from his trance, he mounts with eyes aghast;
When o'er the ship, in undulation vast,
A giant surge down rushes from on high,
And fore and aft dissevered ruins lie:
As when, Britannia's empire to maintain,
Great Hawke descends in thunder on the main,
Around the brazen voice of battle roars,
And fatal lightnings blast the hostile shores;
Beneath the storm their shattered navies groan;
The trembling deep recoils from zone to zone—.
Thus the torn vessel felt the enormous stroke,
The boats beneath the thundering deluge broke;

Torn from their planks the cracking ring-bolts drew,

And gripes and lashings all asunder flew;

Companion, binnacle,* in floating wreck,

With compasses and glasses strewed the deck;

The balanced mizzen, rending to the head,

In fluttering fragments from its bolt-rope fled;

The sides convulsive shook on groaning beams,

And, rent with labour, yawned their pitchy seams.

They sound the well,† and, terrible to hear !

Five feet immersed along the line appear;

At either pump they ply the clanking brake,

And, turn by turn, the ungrateful office take :

Rodmond, Arion, and Palemon here

At this sad task all diligent appear—

As some strong citadel begirt with foes

Tries long the tide of ruin to oppose,

Destruction near her spreads his black array,

And death and sorrow mark his horrid way;

Till, in some destined hour, against her wall

In tenfold rage the fatal thunders fall ;

It breaks ! it bursts before the cannonade !

And following hosts the shattered domes invade :

Her inmates long repel the hostile flood,

And shield their sacred charge in streams of blood:

---

* The *companion* is a wooden porch placed over the ladder that leads down to the cabins of the officers. The *binnacle* is a case which is placed on deck before the helm, containing three divisions: the middle one for a lamp or candle, and the two others for mariners' compasses. There are always two binnacles on the deck of a ship of war, one of which is placed before the master, at his appointed station. In all the old sea-books it was called *bittacle*.

† The *well* is an apartment in a ship's hold serving to inclose the pumps: it is sounded by dropping down a measured iron rod, which is connected with a long line. The *brake* is the pump handle.

So the brave mariners their pumps attend,
And help incessant, by rotation, lend;
But all in vain! for now the sounding cord
Updrawn, an undiminished depth explored. ·
Nor this severe distress is found alone,
The ribs, oppressed by ponderous cannon, groan;
Deep rolling from the watery volume's height,
The tortured sides seem bursting with their weight—
So reels Pelorus with convulsive throes,
When in his veins the burning earthquake glows;
Hoarse through his entrails roars the infernal flame,
And central thunders rend his groaning frame—
Accumulated mischiefs thus arise,
And Fate, vindictive, all their skill defies:
For this, one remedy is only known,
From the torn ship her metal must be thrown;
Eventful task! which last distress requires,
And dread of instant death alone inspires:
For, while intent the yawning decks to ease,
Filled ever and anon with rushing seas,
Some fatal billow with recoiling sweep
May whirl the helpless wretches in the deep.
  No season this for counsel or delay;
Too soon the eventful moments haste away!
Here perseverance, with each help of art,
Must join the boldest efforts of the heart;
These only now their misery can relieve,
These only now a dawn of safety give:
While o'er the quivering deck from van to rear
Broad surges roll in terrible career,

Rodmond, Arion, and a chosen crew, `
This office in the face of death pursue;
The wheeled artillery o'er the deck to guide,
Rodmond descending claimed the weather-side;
Fearless of heart the chief his orders gave,
Fronting the rude assaults of every wave—
Like some strong watch-tower nodding o'er the
        deep,
Whose rocky base the foaming waters sweep,
Untamed he stood; the stern aerial war
Had marked his honest face with many a scar;
Meanwhile Arion, traversing the waist,*
The cordage of the leeward-guns unbraced,
And pointed crows beneath the metal placed—
Watching the roll, their forelocks they withdrew,
And from their beds the reeling cannon threw;
Then, from the windward battlements unbound,
Rodmond's associates wheeled the artillery round,
Pointed with iron fangs, their bars beguile
The ponderous arms across the steep defile;
Then, hurled from sounding hinges o'er the side,
Thundering they plunge into the flashing tide.
    The ship, thus eased, some little respite finds
In this rude conflict of the seas and winds—
Such ease Alcides felt when, clogged with gore,
The envenomed mantle from his side he tore,

---

* The *waist* is that part of a ship which
is contained between the quarter-deck and
forecastle; or the middle of that deck which
is immediately below them. When the
waist of a merchant-ship is only one or two
steps in descent, from the quarter-deck and
forecastle, she is said to be galley-built;
but when it is considerably deeper, as with
six or seven steps, she is then called frigate-
built.

When, stung with burning pain, he strove too late
To stop the swift career of cruel fate;
Yet then his heart one ray of hope procured,
Sad harbinger of sevenfold pangs endured—
Such, and so short, the pause of woe she found!

Cimmerian darkness shades the deep around,
Save when the lightnings in terrific blaze
Deluge the cheerless gloom with horrid rays:
Above, all ether fraught with scenes of woe,
With grim destruction threatens all below;

Beneath, the storm-lashed surges furious rise,
And wave uprolled on wave assails the skies
With ever-floating bulwarks they surround
The ship, half swallowed in the black profound.
    With ceaseless hazard and fatigue oppressed,
Dismay and anguish every heart possessed;
For while, with sweeping inundation o'er
The sea-beat ship the booming waters roar,
Displaced beneath by her capacious womb,
They rage their ancient station to resume;
By secret ambushes, their force to prove,
Through many a winding channel first they rove,
Till gathering fury, like the fevered blood,
Through her dark veins they roll a rapid flood:
When unrelenting thus the leaks they found,
The pumps with ever clanking strokes resound;
Around each leaping valve, by toil subdued,
The tough bull-hide must ever be renewed:
Their sinking hearts unusual horrors chill,
And down their weary limbs thick dews distil;
No ray of light their dying hope redeems,
Pregnant with some new woe, each moment teems.
    Again the chief the instructive chart extends,
And o'er the figured plane attentive bends;
To him the motion of each orb was known
That wheels around the sun's refulgent throne;
But here, alas! his science nought avails,
Skill droops unequal, and experience fails:
The different traverses, since twilight made,
He on the hydrographic circle laid;

Then, in the graduated arch contained,
The angle of lee-way,* seven points, remained—
Her place discovered by the rules of art,
Unusual terrors shook the master's heart,
When, on the immediate line of drift, he found
The rugged Isle, with rocks and breakers bound,
Of Falconera,† distant only now
Nine lessening leagues beneath the leeward bow:
For, if on those destructive shallows tost,
The helpless bark with all her crew are lost;
As fatal still appears, that danger o'er,
The steep Saint George, and rocky Gardalor.
With him the pilots, of their hopeless state
In mournful consultation now debate—
Not more perplexing doubts her chiefs appal
When some proud city verges to her fall,
While ruin glares around, and pale affright
Convenes her councils in the dead of night.
No blazoned trophies o'er their conclave spread,
Nor storied pillars raised aloft their head:
But here the Queen of Shade around them threw
Her dragon wing, disastrous to the view!

---

* The *lee-way* or *drift*, in this passage, are synonymous terms. The true course and distance, resulting from these traverses, is discovered by collecting the difference of latitude, and departure of each course; and reducing the whole into one departure, and one difference of latitude, according to the known rules of trigonometry: this reduction will immediately ascertain the base and perpendicular; or, in other words, will give the difference of latitude and departure, to discover the course and distance.

† *Falconera*, a small island in the Archipelago, to the N.W. of Milo: there is an open space of sea to the north and south of it: but in every other direction are islands at no great distance. The small and steep Island of St. George is situated to the S.W. of Cape Colonna, at the entrance of the Gulf of Egina. Gardalor lies off the coast of Attica, between Cape Colonna and Porto Leono.

Dire was the scene with whirlwind, hail, and shower;
Black Melancholy ruled the fearful hour:
Beneath, tremendous rolled the flashing tide
Where Fate on every billow seemed to ride—
Inclosed with ills, by peril unsubdued,
Great in distress the master-seaman stood !
Skilled to command; deliberate to advise;
Expert in action; and in council wise—
Thus to his partners, by the crew unheard,
The dictates of his soul, the chief referred:—

　"Ye faithful mates ! who all my troubles share,
Approved companions of your master's care !
To you, alas ! 'twere fruitless now to tell
Our sad distress, already known too well:

This morn with favouring gales the port we left,
Though now of every flattering hope bereft:
No skill nor long experience could forecast
The unseen approach of this destructive blast;
These seas, where storms at various seasons blow,
No reigning winds nor certain omens know.
The hour, the occasion, all your skill demands,
A leaky ship, embayed by dangerous lands!
Our bark no transient jeopardy surrounds,
Groaning she lies beneath unnumbered wounds: ˙
'Tis ours the doubtful remedy to find,
To shun the fury of the seas and wind;
For in this hollow swell, with labour sore,
Her flank can bear the bursting floods no more.
One only shift, though desperate, we must try,
And that, before the boisterous storm to fly:
Then less her sides will feel the surge's power,
Which thus may soon the foundering hull devour.
'Tis true, the vessel and her costly freight
To me consigned, my orders only wait;
Yet, since the charge of every life is mine,
To equal votes our counsels I resign—
Forbid it, Heaven! that in this dreadful hour
I claim the dangerous reins of purblind power!
But should we now resolve to bear away,
Our hopeless state can suffer no delay:
Nor can we, thus bereft of every sail,
Attempt to steer obliquely on the gale;
For then, if broaching sideway to the sea,
Our dropsied ship may founder by the lee;

Vain all endeavours, then, to bear away,
Nor helm, nor pilot, would she more obey.".
He said : the listening mates with fixed regard,
And silent reverence, his opinion heard ;
Important was the question in debate,
And o'er their councils hung impending fate.
Rodmond, in many a scene of peril tried,
Had oft the master's happier skill descried ;
Yet now, the hour, the scene, the occasion known,
Perhaps with equal right preferred his own :
Of long experience in the naval art,
Blunt was his speech, and naked was his heart ;
Alike to him each climate, and each blast,
The first in danger, in retreat the last :
Sagacious, balancing the opposed events,
From Albert his opinion thus dissents—
" Too true the perils of the present hour,
Where toils succeeding toils our strength o'erpower !
Our bark, 'tis true, no shelter here can find,
Sore shattered by the ruffian seas and wind :
Yet where with safety can we dare to scud *
Before this tempest, and pursuing flood ?
At random driven, to present death we haste,
And one short hour perhaps may be our last :

---

* The movement of *scudding*, from the Swedish word skutta, is never attempted in a contrary wind, unless, as in the present instance, the condition of a ship renders her incapable of sustaining any longer on her side the mutual efforts of the winds and waves. The principal hazards incident to scudding are generally a pooping sea ; the difficulty of steering, which exposes the vessel perpetually to the risk of broaching-to ; and the want of sufficient sea-room : a sea striking the ship violently on the stern may dash it inwards, by which she must inevitably founder ; in broaching-to suddenly, she is threatened with being immediately over-set ; and, for want of sea-room, she is endangered with shipwreck on a lee shore ; a circumstance too dreadful to require explanation.

Though Corinth's Gulf extend along the lee,
To whose safe ports appears a passage free,
Yet think ! this furious unremitting gale
Deprives the ship of every ruling sail ;
And if before it she directly flies,
New ills enclose us and new dangers rise :
Here Falconera spreads her lurking snares,
There distant Greece her rugged shelves prepares :
Our hull, if once it strikes that iron coast,
Asunder bursts, in instant ruin lost ;
Nor she alone, but with her all the crew,
Beyond relief, are doomed to perish too :
Such mischiefs follow if we bear away,
O safer that sad refuge—to delay !
     " Then of our purpose this appears the scope,
To weigh the danger with the doubtful hope :
Though sorely buffeted by every sea,
Our hull unbroken long may try a-lee ;
The crew, though harassed much with toils severe,
Still at their pumps, perceive no hazards near :
Shall we incautious then the danger tell,
At once their courage and their hope to quell ?—
Prudence forbids ! this southern tempest soon
May change its quarter with the changing moon ;
Its rage, though terrible, may soon subside,
Nor into mountains lash the unruly tide :
These leaks shall then decrease—the sails once more
Direct our course to some relieving shore."
     Thus while he spoke, around from man to man
At either pump a hollow murmur ran :

For while the vessel through unnumbered chinks,. ͡
Above, below, the invading water drinks, . .   .
Sounding her depth they eyed the wetted scale,   -
‚And lo! the leaks o'er all their powers prevail :   ·
Yet af their post, by terrors unsubdued,
They with redoubling force their task pursued.

And now the senior pilots seemed to wait
Arion's voice, to close the dark debate ;
Not o'er his vernal life the ripening sun   .
Had yet progressive twice ten summers run :
Slow to debate, yet eager to excel,
In thy sad school, stern Neptune! taught too well :
With lasting pain to rend his youthful heart,
Dire Fate in venom dipt her keenest dart ;
Till his firm spirit, tempered long to ill,
Forgot her persecuting scourge to feel :
But now the horrors that around him roll,
Thus roused to action his rekindling soul :—

  " Can we, delayed in this tremendous tide,
A moment pause what purpose to decide ?
Alas ! from circling horrors thus combined,
One method of relief alone we find :͏
Thus water-logged,* thus helpless to remain
Amid this hollow, how ill-judged ! how vain !

---

* A ship is said to be *water-logged*, when, having received through her leaks a great quantity of water into her hold, she has become so heavy and inactive on the sea, as to yield without resistance to the efforts of every wave that rushes over the deck. As in this dangerous situation the centre of gravity is no longer fixed, but fluctuates from place to place, the stability of the ship is utterly lost ; she is therefore almost totally deprived of the use of her sails, which operate to overset her, or press the head under water : hence, there is no resource for the crew, except to free her by the pumps, or to abandon her for the boats as soon as possible.

Our sea-breached vessel can no longer bear
The floods, that o'er her burst in dread career;
The labouring hull already seems half filled
With water through an hundred leaks distilled;
Thus drenched by every wave, her riven deck,
Stript and defenceless, floats a naked wreck;
At every pitch the o'erwhelming billows bend
Beneath their load the quivering bowsprit's end;
A fearful warning! since the masts on high
On that support with trembling hope rely;
At either pump our seamen pant for breath,
In dire dismay, anticipating death;
Still all our powers the increasing leaks defy,
We sink at sea, no shore, no haven nigh:
One dawn of hope yet breaks athwart the gloom
To light and save us from a watery tomb,
That bids us shun the death impending here;—
Fly from the following blast, and shoreward steer.
    "'Tis urged, indeed, the fury of the gale
Precludes the help of every guiding sail;
And, driven before it on the watery waste,
To rocky shores and scenes of death we haste;
But, haply, Falconera we may shun,
And far to Grecian coasts is yet the run:
Less harassed then, our scudding ship may bear
The assaulting surge repelled upon her rear,
And since as soon that tempest may decay
When steering shoreward,—wherefore thus delay?
Should we at last be driven by dire decree
Too near the fatal margin of the sea,

The hull dismasted there a while may ride
With lengthened cables, on the raging tide ;
Perhaps kind Heaven, with interposing power,
May curb the tempest ere that dreadful hour ;
But here ingulfed and foundering, while we stay,
Fate hovers o'er and marks us for her prey."
     He said : Palemon saw with grief of heart
The storm prevailing o'er the pilot's art ;
In silent terror and distress involved,
He heard their last alternative resolved :
High beat his bosom—with such fear subdued,
Beneath the gloom of some enchanted wood,
Oft in old time the wandering swain explored
The midnight wizards, breathing rites abhorred :
Trembling approached their incantations fell,
And, chilled with horror, heard the songs of hell.
Arion saw, with secret anguish moved,
The deep affliction of the friend he loved,
And, all awake to friendship's genial heat,
His bosom felt consenting tremors beat :
Alas ! no season this for tender love,
Far hence the music of the myrtle grove—
He tried with soft persuasion's melting lore
Palemon's fainting courage to restore ;
His wounded spirit healed with friendship's balm,
And bade each conflict of the mind be calm.
     Now had the pilots all the events revolved,
And on their final refuge thus resolved—
When, like the faithful shepherd, who beholds
Some prowling wolf approach his fleecy folds,

To the brave crew, whom racking doubts perplex,
The dreadful purpose Albert thus directs :
" Unhappy partners in a wayward fate !
Whose courage now is known perhaps too late ;
Ye ! who unmoved behold this angry storm
In conflict all the rolling deep deform,
Who, patient in adversity, still bear
The firmest front when greatest ills are near ;
The truth, though painful, I must now reveal,
That long in vain I purposed to conceal :
Ingulfed, all help of art we vainly try
To weather leeward shores, alas ! too nigh :
Our crazy bark no longer can abide
The seas that thunder o'er her battered side ;
And, while the leaks a fatal warning give
That in this raging sea she cannot live,
One only refuge from despair we find—
At once to wear and scud before the wind :
Perhaps even then to ruin we may steer,
For rocky shores beneath our lee appear ;
But that's remote, and instant death is here :
Yet there, by Heaven's assistance we may gain
Some creek or inlet of the Grecian main ;
Or, sheltered by some rock, at anchor ride
Till with abating rage the blast subside :
But if, determined by the will of Heaven,
Our helpless bark at last ashore is driven,
These councils followed, from a watery grave
Our crew perhaps amid the surf may save—

"And first, let all our axes be secured
To cut the masts and rigging from aboard ;
Then to the quarters bind each plank and oar
To float between the vessel and the shore :
The longest cordage too must be conveyed
On deck, and to the weather-rails belayed :
So they, who haply reach alive the land,
The extended lines may fasten on the.strand,
Whene'er loud thundering on the leeward shore,
While yet aloof, we hear the breakers roar :
Thus for the terrible event prepared,
Brace fore and aft to starboard every yard ;
So shall our masts swim lighter on the wave,
And from the broken rocks our seamen save ;
Then westward turn the stern, that every mast
May shoreward fall as from the vessel cast—
When o'er her side once more the billows bound,
Ascend the rigging till she strikes the ground ;
And when you hear aloft the dreadful shock
That strikes her bottom on some pointed rock,
The boldest of our sailors must descend
The dangerous business of the deck to tend ;
Then burst the hatches off, and every stay
And every fastening lanyard cut away,
Planks, gratings, booms, and rafts to leeward cast ;
Then with redoubled strokes attack each mast,
That buoyant lumber may sustain you o'er
The rocky shelves and ledges to the shore :
But as your firmest succour, till the last
O cling securely on each faithful mast !

Though great the danger, and the task severe,
Yet bow not to the tyranny of fear;
If once that slavish yoke your souls subdue,
Adieu to hope ! to life itself adieu !
    " I know among you some have oft beheld
A blood-hound train, by rapine's lust impelled,
On England's cruel coast impatient stand,
To rob the wanderers wrecked upon their strand.
These, while their savage office they pursue,
Oft wound to death the helpless plundered crew,
Who, 'scaped from every horror of the main,
Implored their mercy, but implored in vain !
Yet dread not this, a crime to Greece unknown,
Such blood-hounds all her circling shores disown;
Her sons, by barbarous tyranny oppressed,
Can share affliction with the wretch distressed:
Their hearts, by cruel fate inured to grief,
Oft to the friendless stranger yield relief."
    With conscious horror struck, the naval band
Detested for awhile their native land;
They cursed the sleeping vengeance of the laws,
That thus forgot her guardian sailors' cause.
    Meanwhile, the master's voice again they heard,
Whom, as with filial duty, all revered:
" No more remains—but now a trusty band
Must ever at the pumps industrious stand;
And, while with us the rest attend to wear,
Two skilful seamen to the helm repair—
And thou, Eternal Power ! whose awful sway
The storms revere, and roaring seas obey !

On thy supreme assistance we rely;
Thy mercy supplicate, if doomed to die !
Perhaps this storm is sent with healing breath
From neighbouring shores to scourge disease and death :
'Tis ours on thine unerring laws to trust,
With thee, great Lord ! 'whatever is, is just.' "
    He said : and, with consenting reverence fraught,
The sailors joined his prayer in silent thought :
His intellectual eye, serenely bright !
Saw distant objects with prophetic light—
Thus, in a land that lasting wars oppress,
That groans beneath misfortune and distress ;
Whose wealth to conquering armies falls a prey,
Till all her vigour, pride, and fame decay ;
Some bold sagacious statesman, from the helm
Sees desolation gathering o'er his realm ;
He darts around his penetrating eyes
Where dangers grow, and hostile unions rise ;
With deep attention marks the invading foe,
Eludes their wiles, and frustrates every blow,
Tries his last art the tottering State to save,
Or in its ruins finds a glorious grave.
    Still in the yawning trough the vessel reels,
Ingulfed beneath two fluctuating hills ;
On either side they rise, tremendous scene !   -
A long dark melancholy vale between ; *

---

* That the reader who is unacquainted
with the manœuvres of navigation, may
conceive a clearer idea of a ship's state when
trying, and of the change of her situation
to that of *scudding*, I have quoted a part
of the explanation of those articles as
they appear in the Dictionary of the
Marine.
    Trying is the situation in which a ship
lies nearly in the trough or hollow of the

The balanced ship now forward, now behind,

Still felt the impression of the waves and wind,

And to the right and left by turns inclined ;

But Albert from behind the balance drew,

And on the prow its double efforts threw.

The order now was given to " bear away ! "

The order given, the timoneers obey:

Both stay-sail sheets to mid-ships were conveyed,

And round the foremost on each side belayed;

Thus ready, to the halyards they apply,

They hoist ! away the flitting ruins fly:

---

sea in a tempest, particularly when it blows contrary to her course.

In trying, as well as in scudding, the sails are always reduced in proportion to the increase of the 'storm; and in either state, if the storm is excessive, she may have all her sails furled; or be, according to the sea-phrase, under bare poles.

The intent of spreading a sail at this time is to keep the ship more steady, and to prevent her from rolling violently, by pressing her side down in the water; and also to turn her head towards the source of the wind, so that the shock of the seas may fall more obliquely on her flank, than when she lies along the trough of the sea, or in the interval between two waves. While she lies in this situation, the helm is fastened close to the lee-side, to prevent her, as much as possible, from falling to lee-ward. But as the ship is not then kept in equilibrio by the operation of her sails, which at other times counterbalance each other at the head and stern, she is moved by a slow but continual vibration, which turns her head alternately to windward and to leeward, forming an angle of 30 or 40 degrees in the interval. That part where she stops in approaching the direction of the wind, is called her *coming to;* and the contrary ex-cess of the angle to leeward, is called her *falling off.*

Weering, or wearing, as used in the present sense, may be defined, the movement by which a ship changes her state from trying to that of *scudding,* or of running before the direction of the wind and sea.

It is an axiom in natural philosophy, "That every body will persevere in a state of rest, or of moving uniformly in a right line, unless it be compelled to change its state by forces impressed, and that the change of motion is proportional to the moving force impressed, and made according to the right line in which that force acts."

Hence it is easy to conceive how a ship is compelled to turn into any direction by the force of the wind, acting upon any part of her length in lines parallel to the plane of the horizon. Thus, in the act of weering, which is a necessary consequence of this invariable principle, the object of the seaman is to reduce the action of the wind on the ship's hind part, and to receive its utmost exertion on her fore part, so that the latter may be pushed to leeward. This effect is either produced by the operation of the sails, or by the impression of the wind on the masts and yards. In the former case, the sails on the hind part of the ship

Yet Albert new resources still prepares,
Conceals his grief, and doubles all his cares—
"Away there; lower the mizzen-yard on deck,"
He calls, "and brace the foremost yards aback!"
His great example every bosom fires,
New life rekindles, and new hope inspires.
While to the helm unfaithful still she lies,
One desperate remedy at last he tries—
"Haste! with your weapons cut the shrouds and stay,
And hew at once the mizzen-mast away!"
He said: to cut the girding stay they run,
Soon on each side the several shrouds are gone:

---

are either furled or arranged nearly parallel to the direction of the wind, which then glides ineffectually along their surfaces; at the same time the foremost sails are spread abroad, so as to receive the greatest exertion of the wind. The fore part accordingly yields to this impulse, and is put in motion; and this motion, necessarily conspiring with that of the wind, pushes the ship about as much as is requisite to produce the desired effect.

But when the tempest is so violent as to preclude the use of sails, the effort of the wind operates almost equally on the opposite ends of the ship, because the masts and yards situated near the head and stern serve to counterbalance each other in receiving its impression. The effect of the helm is also considerably diminished, because the head-way, which gives life and vigour to all its operations, is at this time feeble and ineffectual. Hence it becomes necessary to destroy this equilibrium which subsists between the masts and yards before and behind, and to throw the balance forward to prepare for weering. If this cannot be effected by the arrangement of the yards on the masts, and it becomes absolutely necessary to weer, in order to save the ship from destruction, the mizzen-mast must be cut away, and even the main-mast, if she

still remains incapable of answering the helm by turning her prow to leeward.

Scudding is that movement in navigation by which a ship is carried precipitately before a tempest.

As a ship flies with amazing rapidity through the water whenever this expedient is put in practice, it is never attempted in a contrary wind, unless when her condition renders her incapable of sustaining the mutual effort of the wind and waves any longer on her side, without being exposed to the most imminent danger. A ship either scuds with a sail extended on her foremast, or if the storm is excessive, without any sail, which in the sea-phrase is called scudding under bare poles.

The principal hazards incident to scudding are, generally, a sea striking the ship's stern; the difficulty of steering, which perpetually exposes her to the danger of broaching-to; and the want of sufficient sea-room. A sea which strikes the stern violently may shatter it to pieces, by which the ship must inevitably founder. By broaching-to suddenly, she is threatened with losing all her masts and sails, or being immediately overturned: and, for want of sea-room, she is exposed to the danger of being wrecked on a lee-shore.

Fast by the fated pine bold Rodmond stands,
The impatient axe hung gleaming in his hands;
Brandished on high, it fell with dreadful sound,
The tall mast groaning felt the deadly wound;
Deep gashed beneath, the tottering structure rings,
And crashing, thundering, o'er the quarter swings:
Thus, when some limb convulsed with pangs of death
Imbibes the gangrene's pestilential breath,
The experienced artist from the blood betrays
The latent venom, or its course delays:
But, if the infection triumphs o'er his art,
Tainting the vital stream that warms the heart,
Resolved at last, he quits the unequal strife,
Severs the member and preserves the life.

CANTO THIRD.

THE SCENE OF WHICH
EXTENDS FROM THAT PART OF
THE ARCHIPELAGO
LYING
TEN MILES TO THE
NORTHWARD OF FALCONERA, TO
CAPE COLONNA IN ATTICA.

Time,

ABOUT SEVEN HOURS;
FROM ONE UNTIL EIGHT IN THE
MORNING.

THE ARGUMENT.

———o———

I. Reflections on the Beneficial Influence of Poetry—Diffidence of the Author.—
II. Wreck of the Mizzen-mast cleared away—Ship Veers before the Wind—Labours Hard
—Different Stations of the Officers—Appearance of the Island of Falconera.—III. Ex-
cursion to the adjacent Nations of Greece Renowned in Antiquity—Athens—Socrates,
Plato, Aristides, Solon—Corinth : its Architecture—Sparta—Leonidas—Invasion by
Xerxes—Lycurgus—Epaminondas—Present State of the Spartans—Arcadia—Former
Happiness and Fertility—Its Present Distress .the Effect of Slavery—Ithaca—Ulysses
and Penelope—Argos and Mycæne—Agamemnon—Macronisi—Lemnos—Vulcan—Delos
—Apollo and Diana—Troy—Sestos—Leander and Hero—Delphos—Temple of Apollo—
Parnassus—The Muses.—IV. Subject resumed—Address to the Spirits of the Storm—A
Tempest, accompanied with Rain, Hail, and Meteors—Darkness of the Night, Lightning
and Thunder—Daybreak—St. George's Cliffs open upon them—The Ship in great Danger passes the Island of St. George.—V. Land of Athens appears—Helmsman struck Blind
by Lightning—Ship laid broadside to the Shore—Bowsprit, Foremast, and Main Topmast
carried away—Albert, Rodmond, Arion, and Palemon, strive to Save themselves on the
Wreck of the Foremast—The Ship parts asunder—Death of Albert and Rodmond—Arion
reaches the Shore—Finds Palemon Expiring on the Beach—His Dying Address to Arion,
who is led away by the humane Natives.

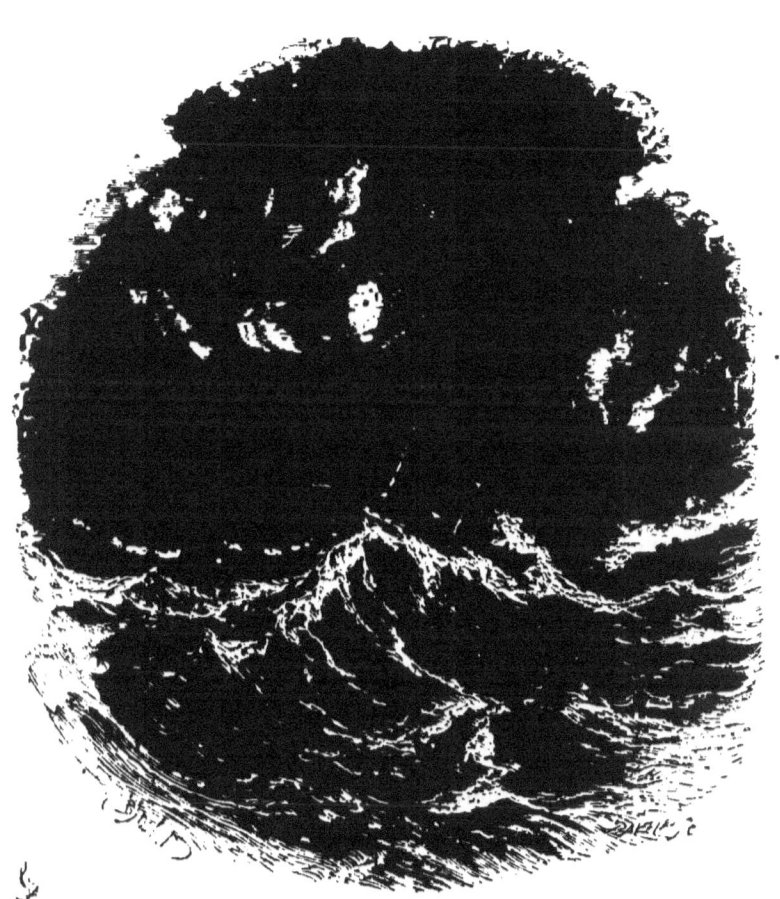

Canto Third.

HEN in a barbarous age, with blood defiled,
  The human savage roamed the gloomy wild;
  When sullen Ignorance her flag displayed,
  And rapine and revenge her voice obeyed;
  Sent from the shores of light, the Muses came
  The dark and solitary race to tame,
  The war of lawless passions to control,
  To melt in tender sympathy the soul;

The heart's remote recesses to explore,
And touch its springs when prose availed no more:
The kindling spirit caught the empyreal ray,
And glowed congenial with the swelling lay;
Roused from the chaos of primeval night,
At once fair truth and reason sprung to light.
When great Mæonides, in rapid song,
The thundering tide of battle rolls along,
Each ravished bosom feels the high alarms,
And all the burning pulses beat to arms;
Hence, war's terrific glory to display,
Became the theme of every epic lay:
But when his strings with mournful magic tell
What dire distress Laertes' son befell,
The strains meandering through the maze of woe
Bid sacred sympathy the heart o'erflow;
Far through the boundless realms of thought he springs,
From earth upborne on Pegasean wings,
While distant poets, trembling as they view
His sunward flight, the dazzling track pursue;
His magic voice, that rouses and delights,
Allures and guides to climb Olympian heights.
     But I, alas! through scenes bewildered stray,
Far from the light of his unerring ray;
While all unused the wayward path to tread,
Darkling I wander with prophetic dread;
To me in vain the bold Mæonian lyre
Awakes the numbers fraught with living fire,
Full oft indeed that mournful harp of yore
Wept the sad wanderer lost upon the shore;

But o'er that scene the impatient numbers ran,
Subservient only to a nobler plan:
'Tis mine the unravelled prospect to display,
And chain the events in regular array,
Though hard the task to sing in varied strains,
While all unchanged the tragic theme remains!
Thrice happy, might the secret powers of art
Unlock the latent windings of the heart!—
Might the sad numbers draw compassion's tear
For kindred miseries, oft beheld too near:
For kindred wretches oft in ruin cast
On Albion's strand beneath the wintry blast:
For all the pangs, the complicated woe,
Her bravest sons, her faithful sailors know!
So pity, gushing o'er each British breast,
Might sympathize with Britain's sons distressed:
For this, my theme through mazes I pursue,
Which nor Mæonides, nor Maro knew.

II. Awhile the mast, in ruins dragged behind,
Balanced the impression of the helm and wind;
The wounded serpent agonized with pain
Thus trails his mangled volume on the plain:
But now, the wreck dissevered from the rear,
The long reluctant prow began to veer;
While round before the enlarging wind it falls,
"Square fore and aft the yards," * the master calls;

---

* The wind is said to *enlarge*, when it | *square the yards* is, in this place, to haul
veers from the side towards the stern. To | them directly across the ship's length.

" You timooners her motion still attend,
For on your steerage all our lives depend,
So steady !* meet her ! watch the blast behind,
And steer her right before the seas and wind."
" Starboard again ! " the watchful pilot cries;
" Starboard ! " the obedient timoneer replies:
Then back to port, † revolving at command,
The wheel rolls swiftly through each glowing hand.
The ship, no longer foundering by the lee,
Bears on her side the invasions of the sea;
All lonely o'er the desert waste she flies,
Scourged on by surges, storms; and bursting skies:
As when enclosing harpooners assail
In hyperborean seas the slumbering whale,
Soon as their javelins pierce his scaly side,
He groans, he darts impetuous down the tide;
And racked all o'er with lacerating pain,
He flies remote beneath the flood in vain—
So with resistless haste the wounded ship
Scuds from the chasing waves along the deep:
While dashed apart by her dividing prow,
Like burning adamant the waters glow;
Her joints forget their firm elastic tone,
Her long keel trembles, and her timbers groan:
Upheaved behind her in tremendous height   .
The billows frown, with fearful radiance bright;

Now quivering o'er the topmost wave she rides,
While deep beneath the enormous gulf divides;
Now launching headlong down the horrid vale,
She hears no more the roaring of the gale;
Till up the dreadful height again she flies,
Trembling beneath the current of the skies:
As that rebellious angel, who from Heaven
To regions of eternal pain was driven,
When dreadless he forsook the Stygian shore
The distant realms of Eden to explore;
Here, on sulphureous clouds sublime upheaved,
With daring wing the infernal air he cleaved;
There, in some hideous gulf descending prone,
Far in the void abrupt of night was thrown—
Even so she climbs the briny mountain's height,
Then down the black abyss precipitates her flight:
The masts, around whose tops the whirlwinds sing,
With long vibration round her axle swing.

To guide the wayward course amid the gloom,
The watchful pilots different posts assume:
Albert and Rodmond on the poop* appear,
There to direct each guiding timoneer;
While at the bow the watch Arion keeps,
To shun the cruisers wandering o'er the deeps:
Where'er he moves Palemon still attends,
As if on him his only hope depends;

---

* *Poop*, from the Latin word *puppis*, is | side forward, beginning at the place where
the hindmost and highest deck of a ship. | the planks arch inwards, and terminating
The *bow* is the rounding part of a ship's | where they close at the stern or prow.

While Rodmond, fearful of some neighbouring shore,
Cries, ever and anon, " Look out afore!"
  Thus o'er the flood four hours she scudding flew,
When Falconera's rugged cliffs they view

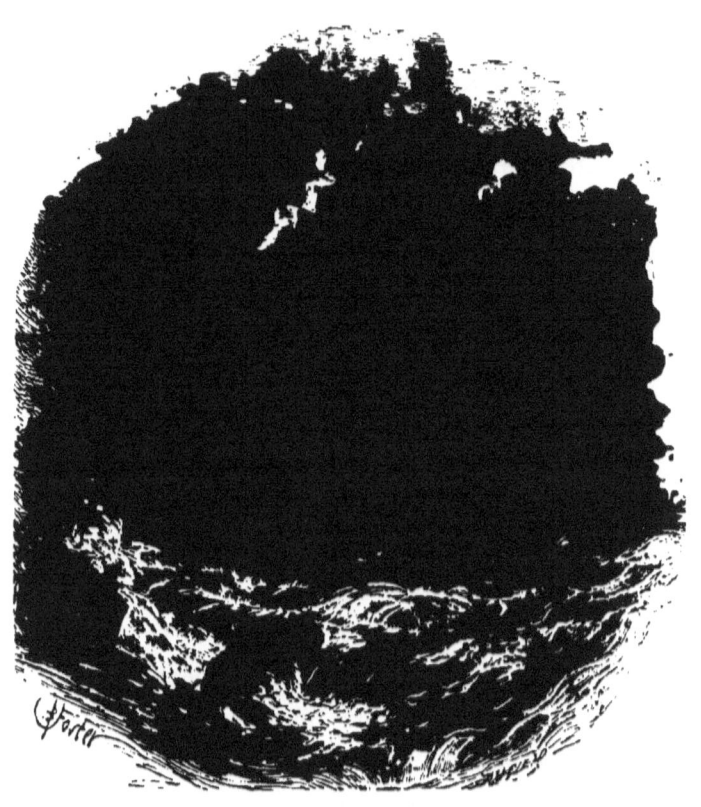

Faintly along the larboard bow descried,
As o'er its mountain tops the lightnings glide;
High o'er its summit, through the gloom of night,
The glimmering watch-tower cast a mournful light:
In dire amazement rivetted they stand,
And hear the breakers lash the rugged strand—

But scarce perceived, when past the beam* it flies,
Swift as the rapid eagle cleaves the skies:
That danger past reflects a feeble joy,
But soon returning fears their hope destroy:
As in the Atlantic Ocean when we find
Some alp of ice driven southward by the wind,
The sultry air all sickening pants around,
In deluges of torrid ether drowned;
Till when the floating isle approaches nigh,
In cooling tides the aerial billows fly:
Awhile delivered from the scorching heat,
In gentler tides our feverish pulses beat:
Such transient pleasure, as they passed this strand,
A moment bade their throbbing hearts expand;
The illusive meteors of a lifeless fire,
Too soon they kindle, and too soon expire.____

III. Say Memory! thou from whose unerring tongue
Instructive flows the animated song,
What regions now the flying ship surround?
Regions of old, through all the world renowned;
That, once the poet's theme, the muses' boast,
Now lie in ruins, in oblivion lost!
Did they, whose sad distress these lays deplore,
Unskilled in Grecian or in Roman lore,
Unconscious pass each famous circling shore?

----

* On the *beam*, implies any distance from the ship on a line with the beams, or at right angles with the keel: thus, if the ship steers northward, any object lying east or west is said to be on her starboard or larboard beam.

They did—for blasted in the barren shade,
Here, all too soon, the buds of science fade:
Sad ocean's genius, in untimely hour,
Withers the bloom of every springing flower;
Here Fancy droops, while sullen clouds, and storm,
The generous temper of the soul deform:
Then, if among the wandering naval train,
One stripling, exiled from the Aonian plain,
Had e'er, entranced in Fancy's soothing dream,
Approached to taste the sweet Castalian stream;
(Since those salubrious streams, with power divine,
To purer sense the softened soul refine,)
Sure he, amid unsocial mates immured,
To learning lost, severer grief endured;
If one this pain of living death possessed,
It dwelt supreme, Arion! in thy breast;
When, with Palemon watching in the night
Beneath pale Cynthia's melancholy light,
You oft recounted those surrounding states,
Whose glory Fame with brazen tongue relates.
  Immortal Athens first, in ruin spread,
Contiguous lies at Port Liono's* head;
Great source of science! whose immortal name
Stands foremost in the glorious roll of fame:
Here godlike Socrates and Plato shone,
And firm to truth eternal honour won;
The first, in virtue's cause his life resigned,
By Heaven pronounced the wisest of mankind:

---

* Porto Leone, the ancient Piræum, received its modern title from a large lion of white marble, since carried by the Venetians to their arsenal.

The last, proclaimed the spark of vital fire
The soul's fine essence never could expire;
Here Solon dwelt, the philosophic sage
That fled Pisistratus' vindictive rage;
Just Aristides here maintained the cause
Whose sacred precepts shine through Solon's laws:
Of all her towering structures, now alone
Some columns stand, with mantling weeds o'ergrown;
The wandering stranger near the port descries
A milk white lion of stupendous size,

Of antique marble; hence the haven's name,
Unknown to modern natives whence it came.
  Next in the Gulf of Engia, Corinth lies,
Whose gorgeous fabrics seemed to strike the skies;
Whom, though by tyrant victors oft subdued,
Greece, Egypt, Rome, with awful wonder viewed:

Her name, for Pallas' heavenly art renowned,
Spread like the foliage which her pillars crowned;
But now, in fatal desolation laid,
Oblivion o'er it draws a dismal shade.
  Then further westward, on Morea's land,
Fair Misitra! thy modern turrets stand:
Ah! who unmoved with secret woe, can tell
That here great Lacedæmon's glory fell!

Here once she flourished, at whose trumpet's sound
War burst his chains, and nations shook around;
Here brave Leonidas from shore to shore,
Through all Achaia, bade her thunders roar:
He, when imperial Xerxes from afar
Advanced with Persia's sumless hosts to war,
Till Macedonia shrunk beneath his spear,——
And Greece dismayed beheld the chief draw near;
He, at Thermopylæ's immortal plain,
His force repelled with Sparta's glorious train;
Tall Oeta saw the tyrant's conquered bands
In gasping millions bleed on hostile lands:
Thus vanquished Asia, trembling, heard thy name,
And Thebes and Athens sickened at thy fame;
Thy State, supported by Lycurgus' laws,
Gained, like thine arms, superlative applause;
Even great Epaminondas strove in vain
To curb thy spirit with a Theban chain:
But ah! how low that free-born spirit now!
Thy abject sons to haughty tyrants bow;
A false, degenerate, superstitious race,
Invest thy region, and thy name disgrace.

    Not distant far, Arcadia's blessed domains
Peloponnesus' circling shore contains:
Thrice happy soil! where, still serenely gay,
Indulgent Flora breathed perpetual May;
Where buxom Ceres bade each fertile field
Spontaneous gifts in rich profusion yield;
Then, with some rural nymph supremely blessed,
While transport glowed in each enamoured breast,

Each faithful shepherd told his tender pain,
And sung of sylvan sports in artless strain;
Soft as the happy swain's enchanting lay
That pipes among the shades of Endermay:*
Now, sad reverse! Oppression's iron hand
Enslaves her natives, and despoils her land;
In lawless rapine bred, a sanguine train
With midnight ravage scour the uncultured plain.
    Westward of these, beyond the isthmus, lies
The long-sought Isle of Ithacus the wise;
Where fair Penelope, her absent lord,
Full twice ten years, with faithful love deplored.
Though many a princely heart her beauty won,
She, guarded only by a stripling son,
Each bold attempt of suitor-kings repelled,
And undefiled the nuptial contract held;
With various arts to win her love they toiled,
But all their wiles by virtuous fraud she foiled;
True to her vows and resolutely chaste,
The beauteous princess triumphed at the last.
    Argos, in Greece forgotten and unknown,
Still seems her cruel fortune to bemoan;
Argos, whose monarch led the Grecian hosts
Across the Ægean main to Dardan coasts:
Unhappy prince! who, on a hostile shore,
Toil, peril, anguish, ten long winters bore;
And when to native realms restored at last,
To reap the harvest of thy labours past,

---

* [This compliment to his countryman David Mallet, author of the beautiful ballad, "The Birks of Endermay," was omitted by Falconer in his third edition.]

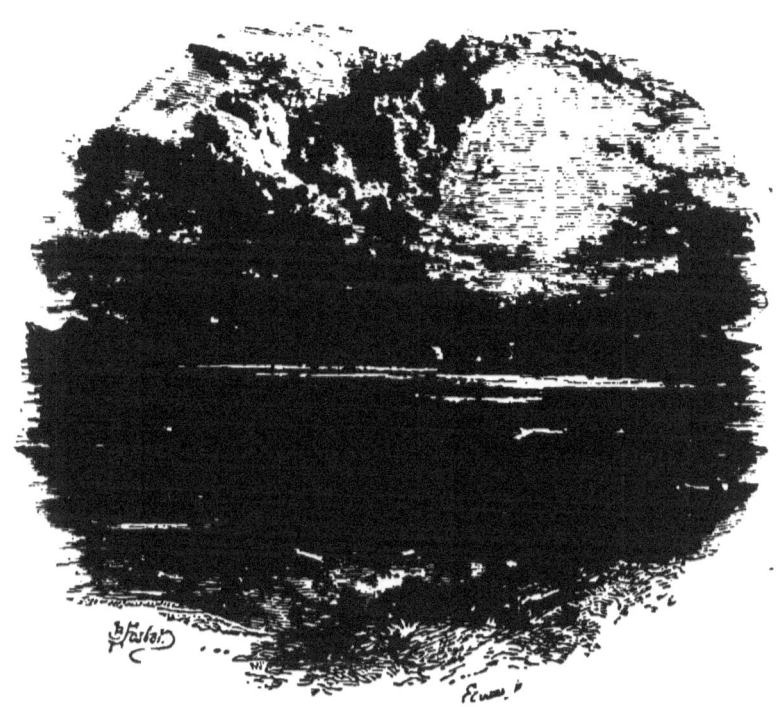

There found a perjured friend, and faithless wife,
Who sacrificed to impious lust thy life:
Fast by Arcadia stretch these desert plains,
And o'er the land a gloomy tyrant reigns.
    Next the fair Isle of Helena is seen,*
Where adverse winds detained the Spartan queen;
For whom, in arms combined, the Grecian host,
With vengeance fired, invaded Phrygia's coast;
For whom so long they laboured to destroy
The lofty turrets of imperial Troy;

---

* Now known by the name of Macronisi.

Here driven by Juno's rage the hapless dame,
Forlorn of heart, from ruined Ilion came:
The port an image bears of Parian stone
Of ancient fabric, but of date unknown.

Due east from this appears the immortal shore
That sacred Phœbus and Diana bore,
Delos! through all the Ægean seas renowned,
Whose coast the rocky Cyclades surround;
By Phœbus honoured, and by Greece revered,
Her hallowed groves even distant Persia feared:
But now a silent unfrequented land,
No human footstep marks the trackless sand.

Thence to the north, by Asia's western bound,
Fair Lemnos stands, with rising marble crowned;
Where, in her rage, avenging Juno hurled
Ill-fated Vulcan from the ethereal world:
There his eternal anvils first he reared;
Then, forged by Cyclopean art, appeared
Thunders, that shook the skies with dire alarms,
And, formed by skill divine, immortal arms;
Here, with the vilest of the empyreal race,
A wretch deformed, devoid of every grace,
In wedlock lived the beauteous Queen of Love;
Can such sensations heavenly bosoms move!

Eastward of this appears the Dardan shore,
That once the imperial towers of Ilium bore,
Illustrious Troy! renowned in every clime
Through the long records of succeeding time;
Who saw protecting gods from heaven descend
Full oft, thy royal bulwarks to defend:

Though chiefs unnumbered in her cause were slain,
With Fate the gods and heroes fought in vain!
That refuge of perfidious Helen's shame
At midnight was involved in Grecian flame;
And now, by Time's deep ploughshare harrowed o'er,
The seat of sacred Troy is found no more:
No trace of her proud fabrics now remains,
But corn and vines enrich her cultured plains;
Silver Scamander laves the verdant shore,
Scamander, oft o'erflowed with hostile gore.
    Not far removed from Ilion's famous land,
In counter-view appears the Thracian strand,
Where beauteous Hero, from the turret's height,
Displayed her cresset each revolving night;
Whose gleam directed loved Leander o'er
The rolling Hellespont to Asia's shore:
Till, in a fated hour, on Thracia's coast,
She saw her lover's lifeless body tossed;
Then felt her bosom agony severe,
Her eyes, sad gazing, poured the incessant tear;
O'erwhelmed with anguish, frantic with despair,
She beat her beauteous breast, and tore her hair;
On dear Leander's name in vain she cried,
Then headlong plunged into the parting tide:
The parting tide received the lovely weight,
And proudly flowed, exulting in its freight!
    Far west of Thrace, beyond the Ægean main,
Remote from ocean, lies the Delphic plain:
The sacred oracle of Phœbus there
High o'er the mount arose, divinely fair!

Achaian marble formed the gorgeous pile,
August the fabric! elegant its style!
On brazen hinges turned the silver doors,
And chequered marble paved the polished floors;
The roof, where storied tablature appeared,
On columns of Corinthian mould was reared;
Of shining porphyry the shafts were framed,
And round the hollow dome bright jewels flamed:
Apollo's priests before the holy shrine
Suppliant poured forth their orisons divine,
To front the sun's declining ray 'twas placed,
With golden harps and branching laurels graced:
Around the fane, engraved by Vulcan's hand,
The Sciences and Arts were seen to stand;
Here Æsculapius' snake displayed his crest,
And burning glories sparkled on his breast;
While from his eyes' insufferable light,
Disease and Death recoiled in headlong flight:
Of this great temple, through all time renowned,
Sunk in oblivion, no remains are found.

Contiguous here, with hallowed woods o'erspread,
Parnassus lifts to heaven its honoured head;
There roses blossom in eternal spring,
And strains celestial feathered warblers sing:
Apollo, here, bestows the unfading wreath;
Here zephyrs aromatic odours breathe,
They o'er Castalian plains diffuse perfume,
Where round the scene perennial laurels bloom;
Fair daughters of the sun, the sacred Nine !
Here wake to ecstasy their songs divine,

Or bid the Paphian lute mellifluous play,
And tune to plaintive love the liquid lay;
Their numbers every mental storm control,
And lull to harmony the afflicted soul;
With heavenly balm the tortured breast compose,
And soothe the agony of latent woes.
The verdant shades that Helicon surround,
On rosy gales seraphic tunes resound;
Perpetual summers crown the happy hours,
Sweet as the breath that fans Elysian flowers:

Here pleasure dances in an endless round,
And love and joy, ineffable, abound.

IV. Stop, wandering thought! methinks I feel their
strains
Diffuse delicious languor through my veins :
Adieu, ye flowery vales and fragrant scenes,
Delightful bowers and ever-vernal greens !
Adieu, ye streams! that o'er enchanted ground
In lucid maze the Aonian hill surround;
Ye fairy scenes! where fancy loves to dwell,
And young delight; for ever, oh, farewell!
The soul with tender luxury you fill,
And o'er the sense Lethean dews distil—
Awake, O Memory! from the inglorious dream,
With brazen lungs resume the kindling theme;
Collect thy powers, arouse thy vital fire,
Ye Spirits of the Storm my verse inspire !
Hoarse as the whirlwinds that enrage the main,
In torrent pour along the swelling strain.
   Now, through the parting wave, impetuous bore,
The scudding vessel stemmed the Athenian shore;
The pilots, as the waves behind her swell,
Still with the wheeling stern their force repel;
For this assault should either quarter* feel,
Again to flank the tempest she might reel:
The steersmen every bidden turn apply,
To right and left the spokes alternate fly—

---

* The *quarter* is the hinder part of a ship's side; or that part which is near the stern.

Thus, when some conquered host retreats in fear,
The bravest leaders guard the broken rear;
Indignant they retire, and long oppose
Superior armies that around them close;
Still shield the flanks, the routed squadrons join,
And guide the flight in one continued line:
Thus they direct the flying bark before
The impelling floods, that lash her to the shore:
High o'er the poop the audacious seas aspire,
Uprolled in hills of fluctuating fire;
With labouring throes she rolls on either side,
And dips her gunnels in the yawning tide;
Her joints unhinged in palsied languors play,
As ice-flakes part beneath the noon-tide ray:
The gale howls doleful through the blocks and shrouds,
And big rain pours a deluge from the clouds;
From wintry magazines that sweep the sky,
Descending globes of hail impetuous fly;
High on the masts, with pale and livid rays,
Amid the gloom portentous meteors blaze:
The ethereal dome, in mournful pomp arrayed,
Now buried lies beneath impervious shade,
Now, flashing round intolerable light,
Redoubles all the horror of the night—
Such terror Sinai's trembling hill·o'erspread,
When heaven's loud trumpet sounded o'er its head:
It seemed, the wrathful angel of the wind
Had all the horrors of the skies combined,
And here, to one ill-fated ship opposed,
At once the dreadful magazine disclosed:

And lo! tremendous o'er the deep he springs,
The inflaming sulphur flashing from his wings!—
Hark! his strong voice the dismal silence breaks,
Mad Chaos from the chains of Death awakes:
Loud, and more loud, the rolling peals enlarge,
And blue on deck the fiery tides discharge;
There, all aghast, the shivering wretches stood,
While chill suspense and fear congealed their blood;
Wide bursts in dazzling sheets the living flame,
And dread concussion rends the ethereal frame;
Sick Earth, convulsive, groans from shore to shore,
And Nature, shuddering, feels the horrid roar.

Still the sad prospect rises on my sight,
Revealed in all its mournful shade and light;
Even now my ear with quick vibration feels
The explosion burst in strong rebounding peals;
Swift through my pulses glides the kindling fire,
As lightning glances on the electric wire:
Yet ah! the languid colours vainly strive
To bid the scene in native hues revive.

But lo! at last, from tenfold darkness born,
Forth issues o'er the wave the weeping morn
Hail, sacred vision! who, on orient wings
The cheering dawn of light propitious brings;
All Nature, smiling, hailed the vivid ray
That gave her beauties to returning day,
All but our ship! which, groaning on the tide,
No kind relief, no gleam of hope descried;
For now in front her trembling inmates see
The hills of Greece emerging on the lee—

So the lost lover views that fatal morn
On which, for ever from his bosom torn,
The maid adored resigns her blooming charms
To bless with love some happier rival's arms;
So to Eliza dawned that cruel day
That tore Æneas from her sight away,
That saw him parting never to return,
Herself in funeral flames decreed to burn.
O yet in clouds, thou genial source of light!

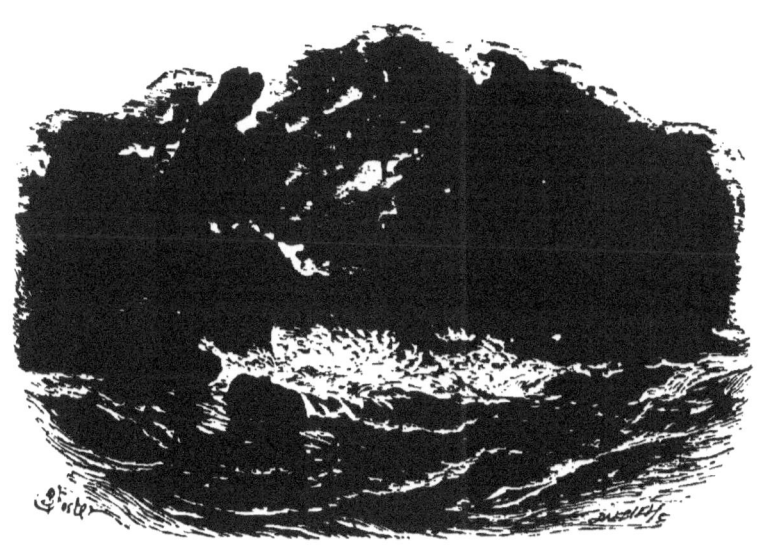

Conceal thy radiant glories from our sight,
Go, with thy smile adorn the happy plain,
And gild the scenes where health and pleasure reign:
But let not here, in scorn, thy wanton beam
Insult the dreadful grandeur of my theme!

    While shoreward now the bounding vessel flies,
'Full in her van St. George's cliffs arise;
High o'er the rest a pointed crag is seen,
That hung projecting o'er a mossy green;
Huge breakers on the larboard bow appear,
And full a-head its eastern ledges bear:
To steer more eastward Albert still commands,
And shun, if possible, the fatal strands—
Nearer and nearer now the danger grows,
And all their skill relentless fates oppose:
For while more eastward they direct the prow,
Enormous waves the quivering deck o'erflow;
While, as she wheels, unable to subdue
Her sallies, still they dread her broaching-to : *
Alarming thought ! for now no more a-lee
Her trembling side could bear the invading sea,
And if pursuing waves she scuds before,
Headlong she runs upon the frightful shore;
A shore, where shelves and hidden rocks abound,
Where death in secret ambush lurks around:
Not half so dreadful to Æneas' eyes
The straits of Sicily were seen to rise,
When Palinurus from the helm descried
The rocks of Scylla on his eastern side,
While in the west, with hideous yawn disclosed,
His onward path Charybdis' gulf opposed ;

---

* The great difficulty of steering the ship at this time before the wind, is occasioned by its striking her on the quarter, when she makes the least angle on either side; which often forces her stern round, and brings her broadside to the wind and sea: this is an effect of the same cause which is explained in the last note of the second canto.

The double danger he alternate viewed,
And cautiously his arduous track pursued :
Thus, while to right and left destruction lies,
Between the extremes the daring vessel flies.
With terrible irruption bursting o'er
The marble cliffs, tremendous surges roar;.
Hoarse through each winding creek the tempest raves,
And hollow rocks repeat the groan of waves:
Should once the bottom strike this cruel shore,
The parting ship that instant is no more;
Nor she alone, but with her all the crew
Beyond relief are doomed to perish too:
But haply she escapes the dreadful strand,
Though scarce ten fathoms distant from the land;
Swift as the weapon quits the Scythian bow
She cleaves the burning billows with her prow,
And forward hurrying with impetuous haste,
Borne on the tempest's wings the isle she passed:
With longing eyes, and agony of mind,
The sailors view this refuge left behind;
Happy to bribe with India's richest ore
A safe accession to that barren shore—
When in the dark Peruvian mine confined,
Lost to the cheerful commerce of mankind,
The groaning captive wastes his life away
For ever exiled from the realms of day,
Not half such pangs his bosom agonize
When up to distant light he rolls his eyes,
Where the broad sun, in his diurnal way
Imparts to all beside his vivid ray,

While, all forlorn, the victim pines in vain
For scenes he never shall possess again.
    V. But now Athenian mountains they descry,
And o'er the surge Colonna frowns on high,

Where marble columns, long by time defaced,
Moss-covered, on the lofty Cape are placed;
There reared by fair devotion to sustain
In elder times Tritonia's sacred fane;

The circling beach in murderous form appears,
Decisive goal of all their hopes and fears:
The seamen now in wild amazement see
The scene of ruin rise beneath the lee;
Swift from their minds elapsed all dangers past,
As dumb with terror they behold the last:
And now, while winged with ruin from on high
Through the rent cloud the ragged lightnings fly,
A flash, quick glancing on the nerves of light,
Struck the pale helmsman with eternal night:
Rodmond, who heard a piteous groan behind,
Touched with compassion, gazed upon the blind;
And, while around his sad companions crowd,
He guides the unhappy victim to the shroud:
" Hie thee aloft, my gallant friend!" he cries;
" Thy only succour on the mast relies."
The helm, bereft of half its vital force,
Now scarce subdued the wild unbridled course;
Quick to the abandoned wheel Arion came
The ship's tempestuous sallies to reclaim:
The vessel, while the dread event draws nigh,
Seems more impatient o'er the waves to fly;
Fate spurs her on!—Thus, issuing from afar,
Advances to the sun some blazing star,
And, as it feels the attraction's kindling force,
Springs onward with accelerated course.
    The moment fraught with fate approaches fast !
While thronging sailors climb each quivering mast;
The ship no longer now must stem the land,
And, " hard a starboard !" is the last command:

While every suppliant voice to Heaven applies,
The prow swift wheeling to the westward flies;
Twelve sailors, on the foremast who depend,
High on the platform of the top ascend,
Fatal retreat! for, while the plunging prow
Immerges headlong in the wave below,
Down pressed, by watery weight the bowsprit bends,
And from above the stem deep-crashing rends:
Beneath her bow the floating ruins lie;
The foremast totters, unsustained on high,
And now the ship, forelifted by the sea,
Hurls the tall fabric backward o'er her lee;
While, in the general wreck, the faithful stay *
Drags the main-topmast by the cap † away!
Flung from the mast, the seamen strive in vain
Through hostile floods their vessel to regain;
Weak hope, alas!—they buffet long the wave,
And grasp at life, though sinking in the grave;
Till all exhausted, and bereft of strength,
O'erpowered they yield to cruel fate at length;
The burying waters close around their head,
They sink! for ever numbered with the dead.

Those who remain, the weather shrouds embrace,
Nor longer mourn their lost companions' case;
Transfixed with terror at the approaching doom,
Self-pity in their breasts alone has room:

* The main top-mast *stay* comes to the fore-mast head, and consequently depends upon the fore-mast as its support.
† The *cap* is a strong, thick block of wood, used to confine the upper and lower masts together, as the one is raised at the head of the other. The principal caps of a ship are those of the lower masts.

Albert, and Rodmond, and Palemon, near
With young Arion, on the mast appear!
Even they, amid the unspeakable distress,
In every look distracting thoughts confess,
In every vein the refluent blood congeals,
And every bosom mortal terror feels;
Begirt with all the horror of the main
They viewed the adjacent shore, but viewed in vain:
Such torments, in the drear abodes of hell,
Where sad Despair laments with rueful yell,
Such torments agonize the damned breast,
While fancy views the mansions of the blest.
For Heaven's sweet help their suppliant cries implore,
But Heaven relentless deigns to help no more.
　It comes! the dire catastrophe draws near,
Lashed furious on by destiny severe:
The ship hangs hovering on the verge of death,
Hell yawns, rocks rise, and breakers roar beneath!
　In vain, alas! the sacred shades of yore
Would arm the mind with philosophic lore;
In vain they'd teach us, at the latest breath
To smile serene amid the pangs of death:
Even Zeno's self, and Epictetus old,
This fell abyss had shuddered to behold.
Had Socrates, for godlike virtue famed,
And wisest of the sons of man proclaimed,
Beheld the scene of frenzy and distress,
His soul had trembled to its last recess!—
O yet confirm my heart, ye powers above,
This last tremendous shock of fate to prove—

The tottering frame of reason yet sustain,
Nor let this total ruin whirl my brain!

    In vain the cords and axes were prepared,
For every wave now smites the quivering yard;*
High o'er the ship they throw a dreadful shade,
Then on her burst in terrible cascade;
Across the foundered deck o'erwhelming roar,
And foaming, swelling, bound upon the shore.
Swift up the mountain billow now she flies,
Her shattered top half-buried in the skies;
Borne o'er a latent reef the hull impends,
Then thundering on the marble crags descends:
Her ponderous bulk the dire concussion feels,
And o'er upheaving surges wounded reels—
Again she plunges! hark! a second shock
Bilges the splitting vessel on the rock:
Down on the vale of death, with dismal cries,
The fated victims shuddering cast their eyes
In wild despair; while yet another stroke,
With strong convulsion rends the solid oak:
Ah, Heaven!—behold her crashing ribs divide!
She loosens, parts, and spreads in ruin o'er the tide.

    Oh, were it mine with sacred Maro's art
To wake to sympathy the feeling heart,
Like him, the smooth and mournful verse to dress
In all the pomp of exquisite distress;
Then, too severely taught by cruel fate
To share in all the perils I relate,

---

* The sea at this time ran so high, that it was impossible to descend from the mast head without being washed overboard.

Then might I, with unrivalled strains, deplore
The impervious horrors of a leeward shore.
   As o'er the surf the bending mainmast hung,
Still on the rigging thirty seamen clung:

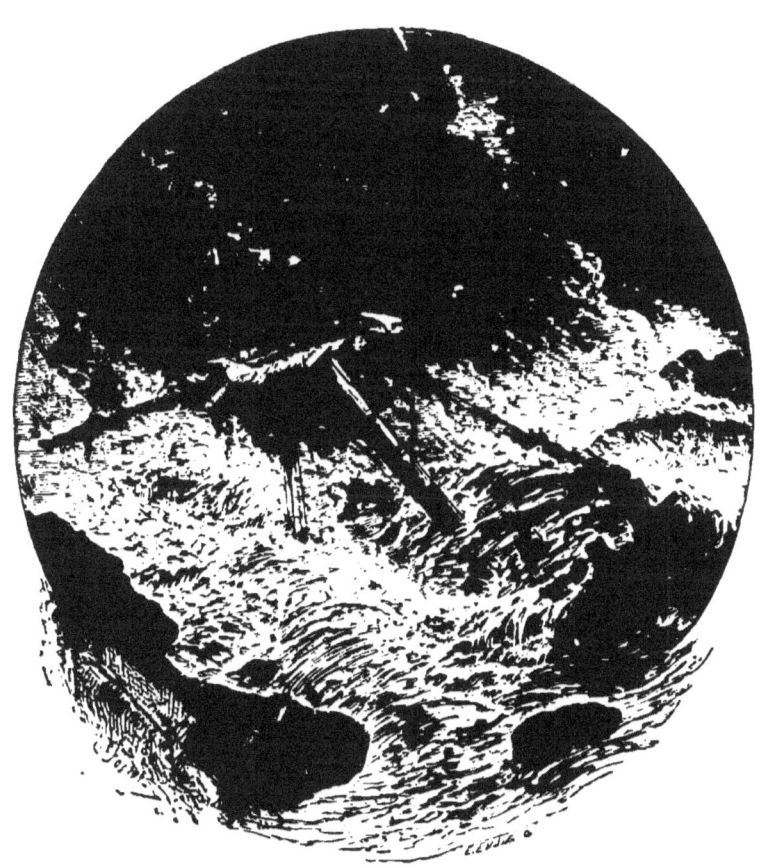

Some, struggling, on a broken crag were cast,
And there by oozy tangles grappled fast;
Awhile they bore the o'erwhelming billows' rage,
Unequal combat with their fate to wage;

Till all benumbed, and feeble, they forego
Their slippery hold, and sink to shades below:
Some, from the main yard-arm impetuous thrown
On marble ridges, die without a groan :
Three with Palemon on their skill depend,
And from the wreck on oars and rafts descend;
Now on the mountain-wave on high they ride,
Then downward plunge beneath the involving tide;
Till one, who seems in agony to strive,
The whirling breakers heave on shore alive :
The rest a speedier end of anguish knew,
And pressed the stony beach—a lifeless crew!

    Next, O unhappy chief! the eternal doom
Of Heaven decreed thee to the briny tomb :
What scenes of misery torment thy view!
What painful struggles of thy dying crew!
Thy perished hopes all buried in the flood,
O'erspread with corses, red with human blood !
So pierced with anguish hoary Priam gazed,
When Troy's imperial domes in ruin blazed;
While he, severest sorrow doomed to feel,
Expired beneath the victor's murdering steel—
Thus with his helpless partners to the last,
Sad refuge! Albert grasps the floating mast.
His soul could yet sustain this mortal blow,
But droops, alas! beneath superior woe;
For now strong nature's sympathetic chain
Tugs at his yearning heart with powerful strain :
His faithful wife, for ever doomed to mourn
For him, alas! who never shall return,

To black Adversity's approach exposed,
With want, and hardships unforeseen, enclosed;
His lovely daughter, left without a friend
Her innocence to succour and defend,
By youth and indigence set forth a prey
To lawless guilt, that flatters to betray—
While these reflections rack his feeling mind,
Rodmond, who hung beside, his grasp resigned;

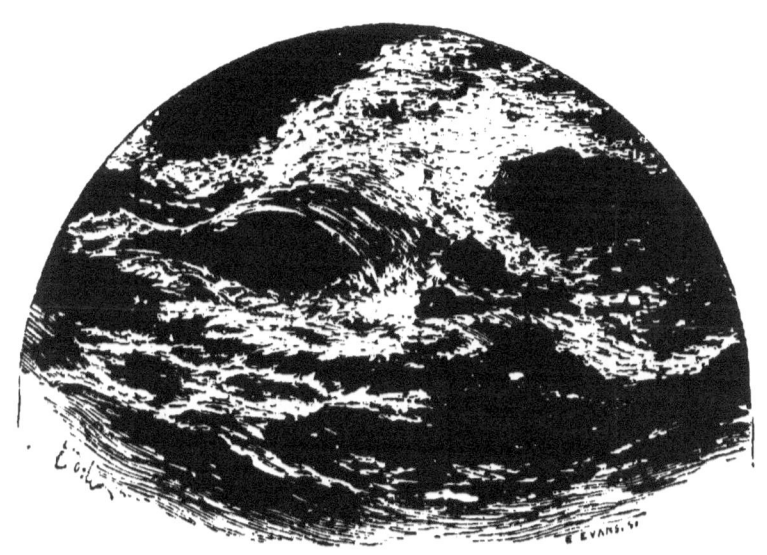

And, as the tumbling waters o'er him rolled,
His outstretched arms the master's legs enfold:
Sad Albert feels the dissolution near,
And strives in vain his fettered limbs to clear,
For death bids every clenching joint adhere:
All faint, to Heaven he throws his dying eyes,
And, "Oh protect my wife and child!" he cries—

The gushing streams roll back the unfinished sound,
He gasps! and sinks amid the vast profound.
    Five only left of all the shipwrecked throng
Yet ride the mast which shoreward drives along;
With these Arion still his hold secures,
And all the assaults of hostile waves endures:
O'er the dire prospect as for life he strives,
He looks if poor Palemon yet survives—
"Ah, wherefore, trusting to unequal art,
Didst thou, incautious! from the wreck depart?
Alas! these rocks all human skill defy,
Who strikes them once, beyond relief must die:
And now sore wounded, thou perhaps art tossed
On these, or in some oozy cavern lost."
Thus thought Arion; anxious gazing round
In vain, his eyes no more Palemon found—
The demons of destruction hover nigh,
And thick their mortal shafts commissioned fly:
When now a breaking surge, with forceful sway,
Two, next Arion, furious tears away;
Hurled on the crags, behold they gasp, they bleed!
And, groaning, cling upon the elusive weed;
Another billow bursts in boundless roar!
Arion sinks! and Memory views no more.
    Ha! total night and horror here preside,
My stunned ear tingles to the whizzing tide;
It is the funeral knell! and gliding near
Methinks the phantoms of the dead appear!
    But lo! emerging from the watery grave
Again they float incumbent on the wave,

Again the dismal prospect opens round
The wreck, the shore, the dying, and the drowned !
And see ! enfeebled by repeated shocks,
Those two, who scramble on the adjacent rocks,
Their faithless hold no longer can retain,
They sink o'erwhelmed, and never rise again !
　Two with Arion yet the mast upbore,
That now above the ridges reached the shore ;
Still trembling to descend, they downward gaze,
With horror pale, and torpid with amaze :
The floods recoil ! the ground appears below,
And life's faint embers now rekindling glow ;
Awhile they wait the exhausted waves retreat,
Then climb slow up the beach with hands and feet—
O Heaven ! delivered by whose sovereign hand
Still on destruction's brink they shuddering stand,
Receive the languid incense they bestow,
That, damp with death, appears not yet to glow ;
To Thee each soul the warm oblation pays
With trembling ardour of unequal praise !
In every heart dismay with wonder strives,
And hope the sickened spark of life revives,
Her magic powers their exiled health restore,
Till horror and despair are felt no more.
　Roused by the blustering tempest of the night,
A troop of Grecians mount Colonna's height ;
When, gazing down with horror on the flood,
Full to their view the scene of ruin stood—
The surf with mangled bodies strewed around,
And those yet breathing on the sea-washed ground :

Though lost to science and the nobler arts,
Yet Nature's lore informed their feeling hearts;
Straight down the vale with hastening steps they hied,
The unhappy sufferers to assist and guide.
  Meanwhile those three escaped, beneath explore—
The first adventurous youth who reached the shore,
Panting, with eyes averted from the day,
Prŏne, helpless, on the tangly beach he lay—
It is Palemon! oh, what tumults roll
With hope and terror in Arion's soul!
"If yet unhurt he lives again to view
His friend, and this sole remnant of our crew,
With us to travel through this foreign zone,
And share the future good or ill unknown?"
Arion thus; but ah, sad doom of fate!
That bleeding Memory sorrows to relate;
While yet afloat, on some resisting rock
His ribs were dashed, and fractured with the shock:
Heart-piercing sight! those cheeks so late arrayed
In beauty's bloom, are pale with mortal shade;
Distilling blood his lovely breast o'erspread,
And clogged the golden tresses of his head;
Nor yet the lungs by this pernicious stroke
Were wounded, or the vocal organs broke.
Down from his neck, with blazing gems arrayed,
Thy image, lovely Anna! hung portrayed;
The unconscious figure, smiling all serene,
Suspended in a golden chain was seen:
Hadst thou, soft maiden! in this hour of woe
Beheld him writhing from the deadly blow,

What force of art, what language could express
Thine agony, thine exquisite distress?
But thou, alas! art doomed to weep in vain
For him thine eyes shall never see again.

With dumb amazement pale, Arion gazed,
And cautiously the wounded youth upraised;
Palemon then, with cruel pangs oppressed,
In faltering accents thus his friend addressed:
    "Oh, rescued from destruction late so nigh,
Beneath whose fatal influence doomed I lie;

Are we then, exiled to this last retreat
Of life, unhappy! thus decreed to meet?
Ah! how unlike what yester-morn enjoyed,
Enchanting hopes! for ever now destroyed;
For wounded, far beyond all healing power,
Palemon dies, and this his final hour:
By those fell breakers, where in vain I strove,
At once cut off from fortune, life, and love!
Far other scenes must soon present my sight,
That lie deep buried yet in tenfold night—
Ah! wretched father of a wretched son,
Whom thy paternal prudence has undone;
How will remembrance of this blinded care
Bend down thy head with anguish and despair!
Such dire effects from avarice arise;
That deaf to Nature's voice, and vainly wise,
With force severe endeavours to control
The noblest passions that inspire the soul:
But, O Thou Sacred Power! whose law connects
The eternal chain of causes and effects,
Let not Thy chastening ministers of rage
Afflict with sharp remorse his feeble age:
And you, Arion! who with these the last
Of all our crew survive the Shipwreck past—
Ah! cease to mourn, those friendly tears restrain,
Nor give my dying moments keener pain!
Since Heaven may soon thy wandering steps restore
When parted hence, to England's distant shore;
Shouldst thou, the unwilling messenger of fate,
To him the tragic story first relate;

Oh ! friendship's generous ardour then suppress,
Nor hint the fatal cause of my distress ;
Nor let each horrid incident sustain
The lengthened tale to aggravate his pain :
Ah ! then remember well my last request
For her who reigns for ever in my breast ;
Yet let him prove a father and a friend,
The helpless maid to succour and defend—
Say, I this suit implored with parting breath,
So Heaven befriend him at his hour of death !
But, oh ! to lovely Anna shouldst thou tell
What dire untimely end thy friend befell ;
Draw o'er the dismal scene soft pity's veil,
And lightly touch the lamentable tale :
Say that my love, inviolably true,
No change, no diminution ever knew ;
Lo ! her bright image pendent on my neck
Is all Palemon rescued from the wreck ;
Take it, and say, when panting in the wave,
I struggled life and this alone to save !—
    " My soul, that fluttering hastens to be free,
Would yet a train of thoughts impart to thee,
But strives in vain ; the chilling ice of death
Congeals my blood, and chokes the stream of breath ;
Resigned, she quits her comfortless abode
To course that long, unknown, eternal road—
O sacred source of ever-living light !
Conduct the weary wanderer in her flight ;
Direct her onward to that peaceful shore,
Where peril, pain, and death, are felt no more.

"When thou some tale of hapless love shalt hear,
That steals from Pity's eye the melting tear;
Of two chaste hearts, by mutual passion joined,
To absence, sorrow, and despair consigned;
Oh! then, to swell the tides of social woe
That heal the afflicted bosom they o'erflow,
While Memory dictates, this sad SHIPWRECK tell,
And what distress thy wretched friend befell :
Then, while in streams of soft compassion drowned,
The swains lament, and maidens weep around;
While lisping children, touched with infant fear,
With wonder gaze, and drop the unconscious tear;
Oh! then this moral bid their souls retain,
All thoughts of happiness on earth are vain!" *

The last faint accents trembled on his tongue,
That now inactive to the palate clung;
His bosom heaves a mortal groan—he dies!
And shades eternal sink upon his eyes.

As thus defaced in death Palemon lay,
Arion gazed upon the lifeless clay;
Transfixed he stood; with awful terror filled,
While down his cheek the silent drops distilled :—
"O ill-starred votary of unspotted truth!
Untimely perished in the bloom of youth;
Should e'er thy friend arrive on Albion's land,
He will obey, though painful, thy command;

---

* ——"sed scilicet ultima semper
Expectanda dies homini; *dicique beatus*
Ante obitum nemo supremaque funera
debet."

OVID, *Met.*, lib. iii.

["But no frail man, however great or
high,
Can be concluded blessed before he
die."

ADDISON.]

His tongue the dreadful story shall display,
And all the horrors of this dismal day:
Disastrous day ! what ruin hast thou bred,
What anguish to the living and the dead !
How hast thou left the widow all forlorn;
And ever doomed the orphan child to mourn,
Through life's sad journey hopeless to complain:
Can sacred justice these events ordain ?
But, O my soul ! avoid that wondrous maze
Where reason, lost in endless error, strays;
As through this thorny vale of life we run,
Great CAUSE of all Effects, THY WILL BE DONE !"

Now had the Grecians on the beach arrived,
To aid the helpless few who yet survived ;
While passing, they behold the waves o'erspread
With shattered rafts and corses of the dead;
Three still alive, benumbed and faint they find,
In mournful silence on a rock reclined:
The generous natives, moved with social pain,
The feeble strangers in their arms sustain;
With pitying sighs their hapless lot deplore,
And lead them trembling from the fatal shore.

OCCASIONAL ELEGY.

THE scene of death is closed ! the mournful strains
   Dissolve in dying languor on the ear;
Yet Pity weeps, yet Sympathy complains,
   And dumb Suspense awaits, o'erwhelmed with fear.

But the sad Muses with prophetic eye
   At once the future and the past explore;
Their harps oblivion's influence can defy,
   And waft the spirit to the eternal shore.

Then, O Palemon ! if thy shade can hear
   The voice of friendship still lament thy doom,
Yet to the sad oblations bend thine ear
   That rise in vocal incense o'er thy tomb.

In vain, alas ! the gentle maid shall weep,
   While secret anguish nips her vital bloom;
O'er her soft frame shall stern diseases creep,
   And give the lovely victim to the tomb.

Relentless frenzy shall the father sting,
   Untaught in Virtue's school distress to bear;

Severe remorse his tortured soul shall wring;
'Tis his to groan and perish in despair.*

Ye lost companions of distress, adieu !
Your toils, and pains, and dangers are no more;
The tempest now shall howl unheard by you,
While ocean smites in vain the trembling shore ;

On you the blast, surcharged with rain and snow,
In Winter's dismal nights no more shall beat;
Unfelt by you the vertic sun may glow,
And scorch the panting earth with baneful heat :

No more the joyful maid, with sprightly strain,
Shall wake the dance to give you welcome home :
Nor hopeless love impart undying pain,
When far from scenes of social joy you roam;

No more on yon wide watery waste you stray,
While hunger and disease your life consume,
While parching thirst, that burns without allay,
Forbids the blasted rose of health to bloom;

[* We have given the Elegy as it appears in the author's latest edition. In the previous impression the following verses (which undoubtedly mar the poetical effect) follow the third verse:—

" From young Arion first the news received
  With terror, pale unhappy Anna read ;
With inconsolable distress she grieved,
  And from her cheek the rose of beauty fled :

In vain, alas ! the gentle virgin wept,
  Corrosive anguish nipt her vital bloom ;

O'er her soft frame diseases sternly crept,
  And gave the lovely victim to the tomb.

A longer date of woe, the widowed wife
  Her lamentable lot afflicted bore:
Yet both were rescued from the chains of life
  Before Arion reached his native shore !

The father unrelenting phrenzy stung,
  Untaught in Virtue's school distress to bear;
Severe remorse his tortured bosom wrung,
  He languished, groaned, and perished in despair."]

No more you feel Contagion's mortal breath,
   That taints the realms with misery severe,
No more behold pale Famine, scattering death,
   With cruel ravage desolate the year:

The thundering drum, the trumpet's swelling strain
   Unheard, shall form the long embattled line:
Unheard, the deep foundations of the main
   Shall tremble, when the hostile squadrons join.

Since grief, fatigue, and hazards still molest
   The wandering vassals of the faithless deep;
Oh! happier now escaped to endless rest,
   Than we who still survive to wake and weep:

What though no funeral pomp, no borrowed tear,
   Your hour of death to gazing crowds shall tell;
Nor weeping friends attend your sable bier,
   Who sadly listen to the passing bell;

The tutored sigh, the vain parade of woe,
   No real anguish to the soul impart;
And oft, alas! the tear that friends bestow,
   Belies the latent feelings of the heart:

What though no sculptured pile your name displays,
   Like those who perish in their country's cause;
What though no epic Muse in living lays
   Records your dreadful daring with applause;

Full oft the flattering marble bids renown
  With blazoned trophies deck the spotted name;
And oft, too oft, the venal Muses crown
  The slaves of Vice with never-dying fame—

Yet shall Remembrance from Oblivion's veil
  Relieve your scene, and sigh with grief sincere;
And soft Compassion at your tragic tale
  In silent tribute pay her kindred tear.